"It's fine, muscular stuff that's both hardboiled and noirish, embodies the best of the 1950s Gold Medal paperback original style, and is therefore a book that comes highly recommended."
—*Mr. Hardboiled*

"This a great book written by an author with clear literary aspirations and an ability to craft a plot utilizing prose far exceeding most of the era's noir stories... a lost classic."
—*Paperback Warrior*

"*Tears are for Angels* is much more than a typical pulp crime book. It tells the story of a man who has fallen into the deepest pits of despair and his struggle back, motivated first by vengeance, and then by love. The novel is fast paced with clever and surprising twists, and plenty of sex and violence."

ads

Tears Are For Angels

Paul Connolly

Black Gat Books • Eureka California

TEARS ARE FOR ANGELS

Published by Black Gat Books
A division of Stark House Press
1315 H Street
Eureka, CA 95501, USA
griffinskye3@sbcglobal.net
www.starkhousepress.com

TEARS ARE FOR ANGELS
Originally published in paperback by Gold Medal Books, New
York, and copyright © 1952 by Fawcett Publications, Inc.

All rights reserved under International and Pan-American
Copyright Conventions.

ISBN-13: 978-1-944520-92-2

Book design by Jeff Vorzimmer, ¡caliente!design, Austin, Texas
Cover art by Barye Phillips from the original Gold Medal
edition.

PUBLISHER'S NOTE:
This is a work of fiction. Names, characters, places and
incidents are either the products of the author's imagination or
used fictionally, and any resemblance to actual persons, living
or dead, events or locales, is entirely coincidental.

Without limiting the rights under copyright reserved above, no
part of this publication may be reproduced, stored, or
introduced into a retrieval system or transmitted in any form
or by any means (electronic, mechanical, photocopying,
recording or otherwise) without the prior written permission of
both the copyright owner and the above publisher of the book.

First Stark House Press/Black Gat Edition: February 2020

Chapter One

I held the sights of the rifle steady on the can. My finger was just beginning the gentle squeeze on the trigger when the old car nosed over the low sand hill. It seemed to hesitate and then came on toward me.

It was a Chevrolet, maybe ten years old, dusty and nondescript, and I couldn't recall seeing it before. Not that many cars came over that hill.

I placed the rifle against the wall of the shack and picked up the fruit jar. It was not half empty yet, but when I put it down it was. I picked up the rifle again and leveled it on the can.

The car was barely moving now. Just as I squeezed the trigger, it came to a full stop. The can leaped on the stick and spun around, its stricken clang fading into the echoes of the shot.

"Nice shooting," the girl said.

I put the rifle down and picked up the jar again and watched her get out of the car. She wore slacks, and as she stepped slowly toward me she hooked her thumbs in the top of them the way a man would. I drank again.

"You're Harry London?"

It was a question, but the asking was not about the name. The words told me she knew I was Harry London. The question was merely a sort of unbelief that the man sitting there in the doorway of an unpainted shack, with a rifle leaning at his side and a fruit jar in his hand, could possibly be the person she already knew he was.

"What about it?" I said.

"They told me what I'd find," she said. "But I didn't believe it. Not till I saw you."

Some brief something that might once have been anger flickered around in my head. I grunted and set the jar down and picked the rifle up again. She was staring at me steadily with large brown eyes. She was a little older than Lucy had been, I decided; maybe twenty-six or twenty-eight. Not more, though, and probably not less.

"Is there anything around here I could sit on, maybe?"

I pointed at the ground, then lifted the rifle to my shoulder again. I hoped that this time the face would be on the can, but it wasn't. I fired anyway, and the can jumped and cried out again.

She was sitting on the ground when I lowered the rifle and I looked at her there, her legs Indian fashion under her, and then she laughed, her voice touched with harshness, her eyes on my left shoulder.

"That's a good trick for you, Harry. Do you ever miss it, just for the hell of it?"

I got up and went into the shack, taking the rifle and the fruit jar with me. I put the rifle in the corner and took a pull at the jar and lay down on the bunk and watched the rough ceiling, a little hazy now, and waited for the face. I tried to shut everything else out of my mind but the face wouldn't come, and then, without looking, I knew she was standing in the door, her thumbs hooked again in the top of the slacks.

"You don't fool me a damn bit," she said. "You're wondering what the hell I want with you, aren't you? And who I am?"

I didn't say anything and she came on into the room and stood over the bunk and looked down at me. Red lips curled in what might almost have been a smile.

"Look at you," she said. "Major Harry London. Gentleman farmer. That's what the papers called you. And now look. You even smell bad."

"Get out," I said.

"I will. When I get ready."

I grunted and let my arm fall toward the fruit jar. She stretched out a leg and nudged it out of reach. My fingers closed down on her ankle.

That hand was strong because it was the only one I had, and I squeezed hard. She made no sound, just standing there on one leg, swaying a little for balance.

"Hand that to me," I said.

"Go to hell."

I squeezed a little harder and she hopped a little on the one leg and then I began to see her, not as someone unwanted and intruding, but as a woman. She had close-cut blonde hair, a little wind-blown, and the large brown eyes were still unwavering, deep-set in her tanned face. The breasts rising under the loose T shirt were not big like Lucy's, but they were high and pointed, and her hips were curved and the skin of the ankle under my fingers was smooth and cool.

I let the ankle go and swung my legs over the edge of the bed. I sat up and looked at her some more. Then I leaned down and picked up the jar. This time she didn't move.

"Get out," I said. "The hell with who you are. Just get out."

Her laugh was sharper.

"I might as well," she said. "But I want to tell you now. I have to laugh when I think about it, the way I felt when I read it."

"Read what?"

"About your wife. In the papers."

I put the jar down again, very carefully, and stood up. I reached out my arm and took hold of her shoulder and turned her around. But she twisted free and faced me again, her face angry now.

"I was looking for something else up in the library at Belleview. And then I read about it, in those old papers. It hit me funny, somehow. And I felt sorry for you. God, for you! You filthy, crazy old man!"

I slapped her hard and she quickly put a hand to her face and gave a little cry. I stepped forward and threw my arm about her waist and picked her up. I felt fists beat at my neck and face and I turned her around and threw her on the bunk and stood over her.

"Don't ever call me crazy," I said. "Not ever."

I think that right then was the only time I ever saw anything that even approached fear in her. She dug back a little into the shucks of the mattress and her hands were raised a little in front of her, her lips parted a little and her knees drawn up, and I guess maybe that faint, slight fear that flitted across her face was the only thing that saved her.

For suddenly it came to me out of what must have remained in me of shame that I stood over her with my one arm raised like a club, my teeth bared through the rank black beard growing from my neck and chin and jaws, my hair falling across my forehead. The tattered clothes I had not washed in weeks clung to my tall, gaunt frame. I reeked of corn whisky, not only on my breath but all over me, and the very air about me was charged with hate.

Then there was fear in me, too, fear of what I might have done, had tottered on the edge of doing. I turned away from her and my arm fell to my side and I went over and sat on the one chair in the room and watched her sit up on the bunk.

"You ought not to have come out here bothering me," I said.

She relaxed a little, and the fear went out of her face.

"I was so damn mad," she said. "It made me so damn mad to see what you'd done to yourself."

"Who are you?"

"I'm a writer. I free-lance for magazines and newspapers. That's why I was interested when I read about you and what your wife did in those old papers. I thought maybe I might be able to work out an article based on it. I thought it had a lot of human interest."

"I don't want anybody feeling sorry for me."

She laughed. "No, you don't," she said. "Then why are you doing this to yourself?"

"You'd better go," I said. "There's nothing here to write about."

"Don't worry. I'm going, all right." She reached down and rubbed her ankle.

"I'm sorry I hurt you," I said.

"Maybe I had it coming. I didn't know your whisky meant so much to you."

"But I'm not crazy. Don't ever think I'm crazy."

She put her head over on one side and looked at me.

"No," she said, "you're not crazy. By the way, do you ever take a bath, Harry?"

I stood up again. "All right, miss. That's enough."

She got up too and came over a little closer.

"It's still there," she said. "Shave off an acre or two of that beard, and peel a few layers of dirt off, and I guess it'd still be the face in the pictures, all right. Even the whisky can't take that jawline away. Only I guess it's not so strong as I thought it was."

I didn't say anything. She looked around her at the unswept floor and then bent over and picked up the fruit jar. She held it out to me, smiling, the brown eyes steady on mine.

"Grab it quick, Harry. I might drop it."

I took it from her and looked at it a moment and then pushed it slightly back at her.

"Have one yourself," I said, "before you go."

Because now I wanted her to stay. I wanted to talk to her and find out more about her.

Because one thing I was positive of: There hadn't been any newspaper pictures of me for her to see. Because I had read every paper that carried the story, searched them feverishly for any between-the-lines meaning, and I knew none of them had run my picture. Lucy's, yes. But not mine.

There was puzzlement in her face now and she pushed her left hand through her hair quickly. She looked at the jar and then back at me.

"That's out of character," she said.

"I'm sorry. Living alone and all, I get pretty touchy."

"I guess you do. Thanks, but no, Harry. I don't think that stuff's for maiden throats."

"It's not so bad. The guy I get it from knows his business."

I held the jar out again and she took it, still puzzled, and I pushed the chair forward.

"Sit down. I'm sorry about all this. And now I'm trying to be nice."

She smiled then and it changed her face all over. It made me smile too, maybe the first time in two years I had smiled at anybody or anything.

She sat down and eyed the bottle and I went over to one of the shelves and poked around and found a glass that hadn't been used. I took the bottle back and poured one, not too stiff.

"There's a spring outside," I said. "I can get you a chaser."

"I'll chance it." She raised the glass to me. "Anything for a laugh," she said, and turned it up.

When she took the glass from her lips, she put it on the floor and leaned forward and began to pat herself on the chest. I laughed.

"I guess you have to get used to it," I said.

"Oh, no! Nobody could get used to that!"

I went over and sat down on the bunk and put the jar down between my legs.

"If you still think there's anything in it for you, Miss …?"

"Cummings. Jean Cummings."

"… Miss Cummings, you can write about me."

"I don't know," she said. "It hasn't got what I thought it might have, I'm afraid."

"What was that?"

"Well, my idea was to play the angle of what a man does after something like that happens to him. Inspirational sort of thing. How a guy makes a new life and all."

"Well, I made a new life," I said.

"You call this life?"

"Life is a lot of things. It depends on what you want out of it."

"And this is what you want?"

"Maybe it's all I can get."

"Hooey. You've still got everything you had in the beginning, only you just aren't using it."

"No," I said. "Not quite everything. An arm, for instance."

"So you lost an arm. And you've been hurt. Who hasn't been hurt? But most people don't just give up and go to pot."

"Most people have got two arms. And people that care about them."

"That's just self-pity."

I couldn't figure what was in her mind, but there had to be something. She was out here for something more than she had told me.

She stood up.

"I don't know why I'm giving you Bible stories," she said. "You must have had friends. You've heard all this before."

"That's right."

"Thanks for the—er, drink, anyway. I better beat it before I get your gander up again."

I stood up, too. There wasn't any way to keep her here if she wanted to go, and so far she had found out nothing except the way I lived, which was no secret. Maybe it was better to let her go now.

She moved toward the door.

"Don't get out that can till I'm out of range," she said.

"I won't."

She looked for a moment as if she would say more, and then she went on out the door of the shack. I stood in the door and watched her go toward the old car.

She walked easily and her hips swayed nicely. Now, when she was leaving, I thought again how it was not to have had a woman in two years. My fingers tingled where they had touched her ankle.

She got under the wheel and the engine ground into life. The car backed a few feet and then she cut the motor and got out and walked around to the other side of it. Then she came back around toward me and I watched her breasts under the T shirt.

"A hell of a note," she said. "A flat."

Something jumped inside of me. "You have a spare?"

"Nope. Not even a jack. You wouldn't have a jack, would you?"

"Afraid not."

She swore, without anger.

"This would have to happen."

"It sure would," I said. "It would have to happen."

Chapter Two

She looked at me sharply.

"What would that mean?"

"Nothing," I said. "Things just happen like that, is all."

"Oh." She looked again at the car. "Well, I have to get back to town somehow. Any busses come by out there?"

"No busses."

"Well, how do you get to town, then?"

"I walk. When I go."

"I'm not up to that. How far is it, anyway?"

"Thirteen miles."

I grinned at her and a little tinge of red began to come down from the roots of her hair.

"You might at least offer to try to fix it for me!"

"I might. If I had anything to fix it with."

"Well, go look at it! Maybe you can do something, anyway."

I lounged away from the door of the shack and walked over to the car and looked down at the tire. I didn't even need to get down on my knees.

The bitch, I thought. The damned bitch. What in hell does she want with me?

"Can you fix it?" She had come up close beside me.

"You know," I said, "it looks as if I'm going to have a guest for the night."

I watched her eyes when I said it, and it was there, all right. But when she spoke, she was good. If I hadn't caught it in her eyes I never would have known that I had said what she wanted me to say.

"Don't be silly. I can't stay here. Couldn't I catch a ride?"

"No cars on that road."

"Then how could I catch a ride tomorrow?"

"Dairy pickup truck. Comes by every morning about sunup."

"Sunup," she said. "My God. You mean I have to spend the night in this hole, then get up with the roosters just because you're not even man enough to fix a simple flat tire?"

It got next to me, even though I knew she had fixed it so she had to stay.

"You got yourself out here," I said. "I didn't send for you. If you have a better idea, let's hear it."

She subsided then and I stood there and watched her, her thumbs hooked in the top of the slacks, chewing a little on her lower lip, the small, high breasts outlined by the T shirt. Then it didn't matter at all that she had a reason, some purpose that couldn't be any good for me, in putting on this show.

She was a woman, and she had everything that had been coming to me in the night, in sweaty, tossing dreams, coming to me, but never all the way, not quite close enough to touch, forever near and beckoning but always just beyond my fingertips. She had it all.

"It won't be so bad. You can have the bunk."

Her nose wrinkled. "I've been on that bunk once. I can make out all right in the car."

I shrugged. "Suit yourself, lady."

She swept her hand through the blonde hair again. "How about some supper?"

"You like beans?"

"Beans are beans. I can take them or leave them."

"You take 'em this time. That's all I have."

"God." She put her head over on one side and looked at me for a long time. "Beans and corn whisky. Is that good for your digestion?"

I walked away from her, toward the house.

"Speaking of corn whisky," I said, "won't you join me?"

She was just behind me.

"If I have to stay here," she said, "you keep off of that stuff."

I swung around and she almost bumped into me. I closed my fingers about her arm and I jerked her up against me and the brown eyes widened and her lips parted.

"All right," I said. "I didn't ask you to get yourself stuck out here. But you're here and you might as well get this straight. These funny cracks about me don't go. I was doing all right till you stuck your nose in, and I'll do all right when you drag your can out of here, which can't be too soon for me. So keep that damn tongue off of me. Just keep that sass to yourself."

Her face was up close to mine, the brown eyes and the red lips, and suddenly I jerked at her again and bent my face to hers. Her free hand came against the side of my face with a stinging wallop and I let her go and we both stepped back.

"And you get this straight," she said. "You keep that filthy hand off me. If you even get those stinking whiskers close to me again I'll let you have it where it hurts the most."

There was a pure, undefiled fury in her voice that told me that she meant it and that she would know how to do it. The brown eyes snapped at me and the words stung right into my ribs.

"Fair enough," I said, and walked away from her toward the spring. "The goddamn beans are in the house when you want 'em."

I walked on, my back to her, but I could feel her watching me. I sat down by the spring, and in a minute she went on into the shack.

Vague worry filled me. She wants something, I thought, she's out here for some reason, and it couldn't be anything else but that. But she couldn't know. Nobody knows.

I leaned over and looked at myself in the still, clear water. The wild beard hung to my chest and my hair had not been combed in days. The tattered collar of the faded shirt was twisted unevenly at my neck.

All right, I thought, I'm no beauty queen. I never was. Let her just keep her damn mouth off of me, is all.

The water looked back at me silently. I let my hand trail in it and then I quickly looked over my shoulder. She was still in the shack. I took my hand out of the water and ran it through my hair and looked back into the spring.

So I'm still no beauty queen. So what?

And then a tide of shame flowed over me and I shut my eyes tightly and leaned back against one of the trees that grew by the spring. Memory rolled up out of the part of me I had locked away and my head began to ache.

Memory narrowed, for no reason at all, and my mind closed in on a Sunday, a shell-pink day when all of the world had been in tune and there hadn't been the face swimming in my brain or the loneliness or the dirt or the despair. It had been our last Easter together, over two years ago.

I had come out on the wide, rambling porch of the house and stood there a moment, waiting for Lucy, looking out across the rich rolling fields that were mine, and I had smelled spring and inside of me something was smiling. Somewhere a bird sang. There were no cars roaring by, no trains whistling and rumbling, no noises at all but the bird and the sound a spring breeze makes in pine trees.

The door opened behind me and I heard her step. I turned quickly and she was pinker, more beautiful than the day, and I went to her and held out my two hands and she took them, smiling. We stood there looking at each other and I was proud of my wife.

"Let me look at you," she said. That was the way she had been. My clothes had always had to be just right, and she had almost taken more pains with my appearance than with her own. She surveyed me then, the white linen suit I had had to have

specially tailored for my lanky frame, the new
Panama, the Oxford cloth shirt, a dark blue tie
knotted neatly under its wide collar, and the brown
and white shoes.

"You'll do," she said. "You look all right for a
lady to go to church with."

"Nobody will notice me," I said. "They'll be too
busy looking at you."

Her blonde hair waved softly around her head,
under a spring hat that wasn't a hat at all, but that
must have been made or grown or created just for
her head alone, under which her blue eyes, smiling
at me, seemed to mirror the very sky. A navy-blue
gabardine suit, exactly matching the shade of my
tie, clung to her full figure, not too tightly, but in
all the right places, and my gaze swept on down
along the slim, lovely legs, and I thought that no
woman in the world could wear high heels like
Lucy.

We got into the Pontiac and went to church, the
breeze and the coming spring and the awakening
blossoms all about us, and I thought that after all
the world was a small place because I could reach
out and touch it, every bit of it that mattered.

I remembered all of that, sitting there against
that tree by the spring, and the thoughts clawed at
me, nameless marauders scaling the wall I had
built around all those old days and nights. Lucy, I
thought. Lucy. Were you thinking about it even
then? Even that day?

I opened my eyes to get away from the images
that darted at me out of the blackness and I looked
in the spring again. Revulsion hit me with solid
body blows and the shame was all over me now, all
through me, and I got up quickly and took two
steps toward the shack.

She was standing there looking at me, across
maybe ten yards of bare sand, darkness nearly on
us now, the shadows from the four abandoned,
lonely derrick posts falling around us and the red
ball of the sun fading slowly to the dunes.

I wanted to hit her, I wanted to beat that smooth face to a bloody pulp, close those eyes forever, because she had seen me like I was, because of the contempt in her face when she looked at me. I stood there, some tremendous swelling coming inside of me, and yet, inexplicably, I did not move.

"I wasn't always like this," I said, my voice a child's, my ears incredulous at my own words.

And then the contempt and the hardness went out of her face, something else filling her eyes, and suddenly I knew she too, whoever she was, was lonely. She had it in her too, the loneliness and the despair and the awful absence of hope. Behind the flippancy and the hardness, something had eaten everything else out of her too.

"I know it," she said. "I know you weren't. Come on and get some beans."

We sat there and we ate the beans, and for the first time in two years I tasted them. Oddly enough, they were good. When I pushed my plate away she was already finished.

"You know what I'm going to do?" she said.

"No telling."

"I'm going to scrub hell out of here. I don't have to stay here but one night, but that's what I'm going to do."

"Go to it," I said. "It's your funeral."

There was plenty of water and a bar of strong lye soap I hadn't used in months and an old rag or two lying around. She rolled up the slacks above her knees and kicked off her loafers. Then she went out to her car and got a kerchief and bound up the short blonde hair and went to work scrubbing the floor.

I had made up my mind to shave after supper, but in order to keep out of the way, I stretched out on the bunk and lit up the pipe I sometimes smoked and watched her.

It was funny. It did something to me. There I was, like any other man, taking it easy after supper, and there she was, like any other woman, doing the housework. Only it wasn't really like that at all. I'm going to get cleaned up, I thought, just as soon as she finishes.

She was almost through before she spoke.

"Tell me about Lucy," she said.

It broke my thoughts abruptly. It reminded me that I still had no idea what she wanted with me.

"It was all in the papers."

"I don't mean about that. I mean tell me about *her*."

It should have made me mad. It wasn't anything a stranger had any call to ask about. But suddenly I found myself talking about my wife.

"She was a blonde like you," I said. "Only her hair was long. It came down to here. She was beautiful."

"I saw that in the pictures."

"Now you, you're not beautiful. You have what it takes, all right, you're good-looking, but Lucy— well, she was beautiful."

"Thanks."

"No offense. Just two different types."

"What was she like?"

"A lot of fun." I thought a minute. "Most of the time, anyway. Sometimes she'd be sort of quiet. Like she was away off somewhere, but it wouldn't last long. She used to say she was absent-minded, but that wasn't it. That last year I guess she was lonely, maybe bored."

"On the farm?"

"Uh-huh."

She laughed. "I wouldn't be. I always wanted to live on a farm." She wrung out her rag in the bucket.

"You? You look like a city girl."

"I am. But I always wanted a farm."

"Lucy hated it. I think she did, anyway. That must have been it."

She got up from her knees and looked at her work.

"That'll have to do, I guess. At least it got the loose dirt." She let the rag drop into the bucket. "Who was the other woman?"

I almost dropped the pipe. "What other woman?"

"The papers said there was one."

"Oh. Yeah." I thought a moment. "None of your business."

She shrugged. "I don't get it, Harry. The way you talk, you're carrying a torch for this Lucy a mile high. I don't get the other woman."

"Me? Carrying a torch? After what she did?"

"It sticks out all over you."

"Listen," I said. "That bitch was—well, never mind. You're out of your mind."

She laughed again. "O.K., O.K. I still don't get the other woman."

"You don't have to. Just let it go."

"Wasn't Lucy any good in bed?"

I got up off the bunk. "That's enough. You just shut up about it."

"So that was it. I'd never have believed it. Not from the pictures."

"Shut up," I said again. I went over to the shelf and picked up the fruit jar. It was almost empty and I finished it in one drink. The hell with it, I thought. The hell with all of it.

"So much for that," she said.

I went over to the trunk in the corner and I got the key out of my pocket and opened it and got another fruit jar.

"Not quite," I said.

I locked the trunk and took the fruit jar over to the door and put it down. Then I went back to the shelf, picked up the empty fruit jar, and started out. In the door, I stopped and looked back at her standing there.

"It's just tonight," I said. "In the morning you go. I'm tired of your damned butting in. So it's just tonight. And for just that long you keep your mouth shut. Or I'll break you in two."

I threw the empty jar against the Cadet heater. It shattered to the floor.

"Clean that up too," I said. I picked up the full jar and went on out.

Chapter Three

I stretched out on the sand by the spring and took another drink from the jar. Then I rolled over on my back and looked up at the stars.

Go to hell, I said to the stars, and then to the moon.

Pretty soon, the pale light in the window of the shack flickered out. Then she came out of the door, looked around for a minute, and saw me, lying there in the moonlight. She looked at me for a long time, but I didn't move or speak.

Then she started off the other way and disappeared over one of the dunes. In a minute or two she came back and went straight to the car and got in. I imagined I could hear the click of the door and then everything was still again. I took another slug at the jar.

I didn't even claim the insurance, I thought, so it couldn't be that. Besides, they'd have been around long ago if they were going to get their noses in it. So it's not the insurance.

And it's not the cops. They aren't interested in it any more. So that leaves only one. Only him.

He's tired of it, I thought, he's tired of the waiting. That must be it. So he's sent her out here to find out what I'm going to do. He could have found somebody like her. He would have known where to find somebody like her to do it for him.

So now I'll have to try again. I'll have to squeeze up the guts and the brains to figure out a way. If I'm ever going to do it. I'll have to try again, after all this time, to figure out a way. Because I don't want him to relax, not ever.

I had to think. That was clear. I had to figure it out between now and morning and get it all straight. I had to think. So I reached out for the jar and took another drink and then another.

Because I couldn't think. I couldn't think any more, not for the last two years. Not when it came to him, and now not when it came to her. I took another drink.

Now his face came, floating somewhere between me and the stars, mocking and sneering, and this time hers was beside it. Now there were two of them and I couldn't do anything about either one, or even think about them.

Pretty soon I was drunk. But the faces wouldn't go away. Then it all went out of my mind and I slept and they did go away. But hers came right back and this time it had a body. It had small, high breasts and thighs and slim hips and I wanted that body, but I could do no more about it than I could do about the face.

When I was awake again there weren't any faces or any bodies, and I rolled over and stuck my head in the spring and drank deeply.

I stood up. My head was a little clearer and I walked over to the car and stood looking through the window at her. She was asleep, sprawled across the front seat, with an old trench coat pulled across her. All I could see of her was the face framed in the fair hair, and her ankles and feet. Her face was calm and unfurrowed and she looked much younger.

The bitch, I thought. But there wasn't any bitterness in it and I went on into the shack and jerked off my clothes and sprawled across the bunk.

Got to think, I told myself. Got to figure it out.

And then I was asleep again....

When I woke it was still dark, and I lay there a moment wondering what the sound was.

It came again, a tiny squeak no louder than a mouse squealing. I was sprawled on my stomach, my legs hanging over the side, and I turned my head very cautiously.

A small beam of light was moving in the corner, and I remembered the key in my pocket and knew it must be the trunk. She had seen me take the key out and put it back.

Very carefully, I rose from the bunk. The whisky fumes were gone from my head now and my senses seemed sharp and clear. I stopped breathing and took a slow step toward the beam of light. In it, I saw a hand moving furtively in the trunk.

I took another step. And another. Then one more. Then I sprang at the faint, dim shape of her.

She went down easily and I was on top of her. The light clattered to the floor and she struggled for only a moment, fists puny against my chest, and lay still, breathing heavily. I caught both her wrists in my hand and sat on her.

"You don't smell any better with your clothes off," she said. There was not even excitement in her voice.

I let go of her wrists and slapped her. I heard the breathing catch, but the voice went on, still calm and even: "I thought you'd be too drunk to wake up."

I slapped her again, this time with the back of my hand, and my knuckles cracked on her jawbone.

Even with my eyes accustomed to the darkness, I could hardly see her. The moon was down and it was that period of intense darkness just before the predawn glow creeps in over the earth.

I found both her wrists again and got up and pulled her with me. I dragged her to the shelf that held the kerosene lamp and pushed her against the wall. I leaned my shoulder against her, feeling the soft breasts under the stump of my arm and the light breath on my ear and neck. I let go of her wrists and fumbled on the shelf for a match, then lit the lamp.

In its uneven glow, I could already see the side of her face turning dark, where my knuckles had struck her. Her eyes were steady on mine. They dropped over me, and what might have been amusement glinted briefly in them.

I flung her across the room and pushed her down on the bunk. She laughed.

"This is getting monotonous," she said.

I turned away and pulled on my pants. Then I pulled up the chair and sat in it by the bunk and reached over and put my hand on her throat.

"You want to live, Miss Cummings?"

She said nothing, but one hand crept to my wrist.

"Because I could choke you to death and bury you out there in that sand before the sun comes up. Don't think I can't do it because I only have; one arm. And don't think I won't do it."

"I won't," she said. "I know you'd do it."

"All right. So you talk. You tell me what you want out of me."

"I told you once."

"You told me lies. About pictures of me that weren't ever printed. About a tire that somebody had screwed a valve stem out of."

I squeezed on her throat a little bit and the fingers tightened on my wrist.

"What is it you're after? Did he send you?"

"Did who?"

"What's he want you to find out?"

She shook her head. "Honest to God, I don't know what you're talking about."

"Then how about the trunk?"

"I wanted to know more about you and Lucy. I thought maybe there'd be something else there."

"You were wrong."

She shrugged and took her hand off my wrist. "It was a chance."

"All right, Miss Cummings. You came out here butting in of your own free will. You got a black eye for your trouble and you're damn lucky to get off that light. Now let's you fish up that valve stem and clear out of here."

She laughed. "I'll be glad to. I'll get out of here so fast it'll make your head swim."

"And take him a message. Tell him this from me. Tell him I said just to keep waiting. And tell him not to get in an uproar. It won't be long now."

No, I thought, it won't be long. Because now there isn't any other way and I'll just have to walk in there and let him have it right in the gizzard. The hell with the rest of it now. The hell with them finding out. That way is better than nothing.

She was looking at me with her brows drawn in puzzlement. I took my hand off her throat.

"Tell who that? And what won't be long?"

She was good, all right. For just a second she had me believing it. But for only a second.

"Lover boy," I said. "Stewart."

She shook her head. "I don't know any Stewart."

Nobody could act like that, I thought. Maybe ... But it had to be that way.

"Cut it out," I said.

"Look, I don't know any Stewart. I don't know anything about what you're saying. I was never even in this state before this week."

I sat there and looked at her and I knew she was telling the truth. She was leaning up on one elbow and there was honest bewilderment written all over her face.

"Honest to God," she said again.

"Then it doesn't make any sense. If he didn't send you, why did you come?"

"Listen, I'm leaving, I'm going. Why don't you just let me get up and go, and forget about me? Get on back to your bottle and your rifle and just let me go."

She was pleading with me now, for the first time, and the sincerity was gone out of her face. And then I knew that whatever it was she had come for, she had found. Because now she wanted to get out. She wanted to get away from there, after she had worked so hard to stay.

"Please," she said.

"No. You better stay a while longer."

"Why?"

And, without any conscious will to do so, I thought of a good reason.

I put my hand on her right breast and squeezed gently.

"I haven't felt that in two years," I said.

At first, she clawed at my wrist. Then she leaned up a little bit and swung at my face and I took my hand away and blocked the punch.

I stood up, and as she tried to rise, I pushed her back on the bunk. Then I was on it with her and feeling for the neckline of the T shirt.

She was a coiled spring of fury. I felt fingernails rake at my arms and face, and teeth in my neck. But I caught the T shirt and yanked it away.

"Get off of me!" I heard it coming at me in a raging whisper and I laughed and tore at the straps of her brassiere. They gave easily and my hand fumbled at her breasts again. This time they were bare.

I had no other arm. There was only my body to hold her down, and now she rolled under me and I went against the wall and she got away and sprang to the middle of the room. I cursed the useless stump hanging from my shoulder, and in one continuous motion I was on the floor too and we faced each other in the dim lamplight of the room.

She stood there, not even trying to cover the bare breasts. They were even smaller than I had thought, and they were stark white against the deep tan of her neck. Her hair was wild and the brown eyes blazed at me.

I took a step forward. Instead of retreating, she came lunging at me, her breath heaving, and I grabbed at her. She squirmed free and aimed a kick between my legs. I jumped back and the backs of my legs struck the bunk and I sat down abruptly.

She could have run then, but she swung wildly with her fist. I moved my head to one side and caught her arm and pulled her across my lap and crushed my lips down on hers. She struggled furiously and I took my head away and her eyes glared into mine.

"You can do it," she said, "I know you can. But it won't do you any good, you bastard!"

I grinned at her. I felt more alive than I had in two years and I knew I had to have her. I had to have a woman like that, who could have run but who had kept on fighting back.

I hugged her tightly now so that only her legs could move and she could not reach me with a kick. Her breasts pushed against my bare chest.

"Why won't it do me any good?"

"Because you can't stop me that way. You'll have to kill me to stop me. Like you killed Lucy."

Chapter Four

For a moment, I didn't move. Then I pushed her away from me. She hit the floor with a bump and gave a little cry and lay there looking at me.

I ran.

I sprang across her and out the door of the little house and I ran, on and on, across the dunes. I ran till my whisky-shortened breath caught in my throat and sharp knives pierced my ribs. I staggered on a little farther and sprawled out in the sand and put my head on my arm and shook.

After a while it passed and I rolled over on my back.

She knows, I thought. She knows I killed Lucy.

And it came to me then with startling force how I had been living with the horror of it these two years, how I had pushed it into the remote corners of my mind and saturated it with the whisky and the hate and the self-pity and the loneliness until I didn't even know it was there. But it was there, coiled, waiting, ready, and then an unknown girl had touched it, released the spring, and it had come shooting out of my mind at me, rocket-driven horror.

But she couldn't know, I thought. She couldn't! Nobody knows but Stewart and me. And she doesn't know Stewart.

So I had to get up then and go back, go back to find out what she knew and how she had learned it and to tell her how it had been. The horror of it, at last released, could not be borne alone. That was the main thing. I had to go back to tell her how it had been. I had to share it now, after the years of hiding, I had to tell it to someone.

I kept listening for the car to start. I remembered the tire. It would take some time to put the stem in and get it pumped up. And sure enough, she was working away with the pump when I came over the last dune.

I came silently up behind her, my bare feet silent in the soft, night-cooled sand, and watched her bending with the pump. She had the T shirt pinned around her now, and its tail fluttered with her movements.

"What makes you think I killed her?" I said.

There was the slightest jerk in the rhythm of the pumping. Then she went on with it, steadily, as if no word had been spoken.

"You owe me a bra," she said. "That was my best one."

"How did you know about it?"

She didn't say anything.

"I'm not going to hurt you."

She stopped pumping and kicked at the tire. Then she went back to the work.

"What are you going to do?"

"Go to the police."

There was no emotion in the voice. It was simply a flat statement of purpose.

"All right," I said. "Let me tell you how it was first."

"I know you killed her. And I know you. That's enough for me."

"It was an accident."

"Prove that to the police."

"I'm not trying to stop you from telling them. I just want you to know how it was. I've got to tell somebody. I can't live with it any more."

The pumping was finished then. She kicked the tire again and knelt down and began to unscrew the hose from the valve.

"All I'm interested in is that she's dead and you killed her. She was … a friend of mine."

"Lucy?"

She didn't say anything. She picked up the pump, opened the car door, and started to slide in the seat. Then she looked at me again, still standing barefooted in the sand. The side of her face was quite dark now, the purplish bruise accusing and shameful.

"It didn't happen the way the papers had it," she said. "I know it didn't. Maybe I can't prove it, but I can try."

"And you're sure I did it?"

"Yes. I'm sure."

I stepped forward then and I put out my hand to touch her arm. But she moved it, and I let my hand fall.

"If you knew her," I said, "you ought to want to hear how she died."

She laughed, hard and brittle in the darkness.

"All right," she said. "There's plenty of time, I guess. I've already waited two years."

I sat down on the sand and she turned in the car seat and put her feet on the running board and her elbows on her knees. The car door swung gently against her legs.

"I had started down to the coast on a fishing trip, late one afternoon. I got about halfway down there, but then it began to come up a storm...."

I didn't really mind. I had looked forward to that trip for some time, but now, when I was actually on the way, I began to miss Lucy. So I turned around and started home.

That was a real storm. The rain drove hard against the windshield and there were thunder and lightning, like giant Roman candles, and I began to have trouble seeing the road. But I was going home to Lucy, the flat, rain-washed ribbon of pavement in front of me was taking me to her, and I thought, To hell with the storm. To hell with fishing, too.

I remembered the way she had clung to me when I had left that afternoon, as if she might never see me again. I felt my pulse throb at the memory of her body pressed to mine and I stepped harder on the gas pedal.

It was late when the headlights picked up the dirt road leading off to the right, leading to the old-fashioned farmhouse where Lucy was waiting. She won't even be in bed yet, I was thinking, maybe reading or playing one of those damned card games she likes. I braked carefully and made the turn and felt the wheels, less sure now, on the rain-soaked earth.

The London place—that's what county folks call it—is less than a mile from the highway, a low, rambling old house, white-painted, with a porch running around three sides. It's one-storied, set back in a grove of trees.

My father left the place to me and his father to him and so on back to the first London, whoever he was, who cleared the land and put in tobacco. When I sold it, it had the biggest tax valuation in Coshocken County.

The Pontiac nosed cautiously into the drive. The house was dark, and I decided Lucy must be in bed after all. I braked to a stop by the house, rather than going on back to the barn. From here it was only two jumps to the unrailed porch and I would not get so wet.

In the darkness outside the car, I could see the pale reflection of water standing on the ground, and I swore. I had stopped right in the middle of a large puddle.

I glanced around the cluttered interior of the car. I can bring all this stuff in tomorrow, I thought. I swung around, lifted my feet to the seat, and quickly untied mv shoes. Carrying them in my hand, the heavy socks stuffed down in the toes, I opened the door of the Pontiac and leaped through the rain to the porch.

In the instant it took me to gain the shelter, I became soaked through. I stood now, breathing quickly with the sudden movement, on the side of the house opposite from that where our bedroom was located.

It opened onto the same gallery-like porch on which I now stood. The rain beat in under the low, wide eaves.

I walked silently along the porch, the bare pad of my feet on the planking lost in the drive of the rain. I turned the corner to the front of the house, and as I did so I was instantly aware of a thin, pale glow, an atmosphere rather than a beam of light, from around the far corner of the house.

Quick pleasure thrilled in me. She's still awake, I thought. Reading in bed, like as not. Except for the living room, the bedroom was the only room opening onto the porch. The light could only come from there.

For a moment, in stark animal pleasure and pride and greed, I knew how she would look, propped up in the wide four-poster, sunk in the deepness of the feather mattress, her knees drawn up before her, the book, a mystery, or a movie magazine, on her knees, the coverlet only to her waist against the rain chill, the pale, mellow gold of her hair about the pink-white curve of shoulder and arm and breast, the lips parted and the eyes avid on the page, but all of her eager, waiting, not expecting, but still waiting anyway for my return, for me to come home to her.

I want to see it, I thought, I want to see her that way and her not know it and then go in to her with it inside of me, and her still not knowing I have seen her that way, and take her to me and feel her in my arms.

Quickly now, I turned the corner of the porch and silently moved down its length to the lighted window. The shade was half pulled and I went easily to my knees and put the shoes down softly beside me and peered in through the window.

In that first second of glancing, a million years peeled away from me and left me naked, all the sum of civilization piled at my knees where it had fallen. No thoughts, no dreams, no fears, no pride, not even physical pain, but only raw fury rose in me as I crouched on the damp porch.

My legs straightened and I was on my feet, moving forward as if I would surge through the interfering glass. But some instinct reached up from the heapings at my feet and caught at me and my arms dropped to my side and I stood there, half stooping, my arms dangling, my fists lax and free, and watched them through the window.

They were on the bed, Lucy and the man whose face I could not see, only his naked, ugly rump and his back and his shoulders, clutched together, writhing together, primal in their attitude. Lucy's face was visible over the hairy shoulder, the eyes closed, the mouth open, the whole face grimaced, and the hair the same mellow paleness I remembered, but not clouding to her shoulders now, but plunging straight and lank to the whiteness of the bed.

The man's head lifted momentarily, almost abruptly, and was down again. But it was enough for me to see, to know, and shame flowed in me with ravaging power at the sight of him there with her, and I turned and walked again along the porch, my fists clenched now, feeling in me again, and hate, red hate, rolling up with the rage and the shame to my brain.

Silently I entered the front door. I moved across the old rug to the high-backed desk, opened its center drawer, and took from it the pistol, and closed the drawer again and moved away, down the hall toward the bedroom and the two of them straining together there.

I did not check the pistol's chamber. It was always loaded. I put my hand to the doorknob and opened the door and stood there in the hall, watching a widening view of the room past the slowly opening door, their heads first, then their bodies, then the rest of the room, the light from the single lamp flooding over me now as I stood, feet wide, the pistol dangling in my right hand.

They had finished now and lay unmoving. Somehow, this was the final and absolute, the incredible peak of their crime. To lie as I myself had so often lain with her, weak and empty and warm, all of my love poured out into her and all of hers risen to meet it, to take it, to encompass it, with the warmth and the knowledge sweet inside of me that she was mine and I was hers—that was the part of it I could not bear anyone else having. The other part was instinctual, animal; but this was the human part of it, and by having it too, this man had taken it from me forever.

I raised the gun and placed the sight on his head. At that moment her head swiveled, and she looked at me and I saw the quick movement and then our eyes met. I lashed her with hate and scorn and shame and rage; she lashed me with fear and despair and wild, disbelieving horror.

Chapter Five

She screamed then, and the man rolled swiftly over to look toward the door and saw me and the gun. He yelled too, not a scream, but a quick, short shout, surprise and fear mingled in it, but not terror, not horror, Not yet.

He put his feet to the floor and sat up, his motions even and slow, as if not wanting to scare a nervy horse, and his voice was very gentle as he spoke:

"You got a right to shoot, Harry."

"No! Oh, Harry, no!"

She was crouched beside him on the bed then, her eyes stricken with pleading and fear, her hair wild now, and her breasts which had always thrust forward, a little too large, but high and firm and stirring, now sagging, her skin not pink-white, but stark white, and her mouth dry and narrow and old, not curving, alive, red.

"Listen, Harry. You can't. Let me tell you, Harry—"

I took a step forward and her voice stopped, abruptly, on the same note, and oddly I was aware again of my soaked, clinging clothes, somehow more obscene than their absolute nudity.

"Did you whisper in his ear? Like you do in mine?"

I had not known I would say it until the voice, surely not my own, rasped in the stillness.

Her hand went to her throat, the white rounded arm covering one breast, the other curiously out of place without its mate, her stomach pulled flat with a sharp intake of breath.

"Look, Harry." The man's voice was still gentle. "Take it easy. You got a right to shoot me. Sure you have. But think a minute, Harry—"

"Shut up." I didn't take my eyes from Lucy.

"Did you say those things you always say, those words you use? Did you do that, too?"

Thought was coming back to me, thought to go with the pain and shame and fury, and it was the more intolerable because of the thinking. This can't be happening, I thought. None of it is true. It will go away with the rain. It can't be happening to me, to Harry London.

Lucy was speaking now, quickly, her voice harsh, the charm and the allure gone out of her, and only the nakedness and the fear left.

"I can tell you how it was, Harry! He made me do it … he forced me. Please, please, don't look at me that way until I tell you about it, Harry!"

"I won't shoot you," I said. "You don't have to beg. Just him. Just Stewart."

"Listen to me," Stewart said. "You're mad. You're hurt. I don't blame you. But shooting me won't help, it won't do any good. You'll go to the chair for it, Harry."

I laughed. "The chair," I said. I laughed again. "In this county? For killing a guy I catch with my wife?"

"It's murder."

"Murder is a word. Murder is when you killed somebody, the word they use. Murder's not when you step on a snake."

"Harry, please," Lucy said. "Don't make it worse. If you'd only listen …"

"I used to laugh about you, Stewart. We all did. The Great Lover, we called you. We wondered how long you could get away with your tomcatting without getting shot. And now I know. Now I know."

Suddenly, their nudity together was an obscenity not to be borne. "You." I flicked the gun at Stewart. "Get your clothes on."

He stood up, slowly, easily, fear still in his eyes, but not yet panic. I could figure him, how he was still thinking, still figuring, knowing there was a way out, that he only had to find it, the path, the words that would get him out of it. I saw it all in the darkly handsome face, the blue eyes, the set of the broad shoulders.

I looked down at him, nearly five inches shorter than I was. I stand six feet five inches in my socks. I looked down at the swart, handsome man who had destroyed my world and I calculated, coolly and malevolently, and decided to kill, for the first time decided to kill, after feeling, absorbing, accepting the instinct, the urge, but staying my hand.

In cool, calm hatred I made up my mind to kill Dick Stewart.

"Never mind your damn drawers," I said. "Just get your britches on. I don't want you to look too pretty."

He fumbled a little with his slacks, almost stumbled as he thrust a leg into them. I'm getting to him now, I thought; he's beginning to choke up. It's hitting him now. Pleasure squeezed me all over, then. His eyes never left the gun.

Lucy's voice raced at me, rising, falling, pleading with me. I didn't hear any of it. I looked at her and her face was streaked with tears and she shrank toward the foot of the bed, her hand groping toward her robe.

She picked it up and in two strides I was at her side and tore it from her. I flung it against the wall.

"Harry!"

"You got nothing to hide," I said.

"Harry, please. If you'll only listen …"

I flicked the gun at him again.

"Besides," I said, "I want him to be looking at you. I want you to be the last thing he sees. Just the way he made you."

Her hands flew to her head and she was weeping then, sobbing loudly and unbeautifully, and her eyes begged me and I grinned at her and felt my skin split back across my teeth. I kept looking at him, his back against the wall now, terror at last coming into his face, and I talked to her, but I wanted the words to nail into him like spikes.

"You can explain," I said. "Sure you can. How it was just a little accommodation. How he just gave you a little while I wasn't here to do it. How it didn't mean a thing to you. All right. I believe it. And since it didn't mean a thing to you, you won't mind if I kill him. Will you?"

"You got it all wrong, Harry. I swear it." His words chased one another, flat, quick, tumbling from him like the rain falling outside. "I was fishing back at the creek and my car drowned out, see, and I came to use your phone and I knocked and she let me in and she didn't have on anything but that robe there and I—"

"That's a lie!" she screamed. "That's not so, Harry! He's been after me and bothering me until I thought I'd go crazy and then he said—"

"Shut up!" She was half off the bed now, one foot resting on the floor, her eyes wild, pleading. "Aren't you a pretty pair?" I said. "Aren't you something? The bed's not cool yet and look at you now. Just look at you."

The almost funny part was that I was beginning to enjoy myself.

My wife was sitting there naked on the bed, her breasts mocking reminders of another man's hands, her whole body a possession now of his too, her wild eyes and long, lank hair a far cry from the allure I had once known, begging me to believe she could not help lying in my bed with another man. That very other man stood there barefoot against the wall, his trousers sagging at his hips, the dust of the floor where he had cast them still clinging to them, his body sweating, not only with fear but still with his straining to her, shouting at me that my wife had deliberately lured him into that same bed upon which she now sat, naked and lewd and alone in terror.

And I was enjoying it. I was enjoying venting upon them the rage at my dispossession, the hurt

at my betrayal, and the shame at my cuckoldry at
the hands of a man whose habits with other men's
wives and daughters was a standing joke in every
crossroads store and filling station in the county.

Or rather, there was someone who inhabited
my sopping clothes, and who held the pistol I had
brought home from the war, who stood in that room
and laughed at the terror of them and the misery
of me, who watched it all and laughed, and shut
away inside himself that part of it which he knew
even then would someday arise to turn his dreams
to nightmares and his thoughts to tortures.

It wasn't I that enjoyed it. But it was someone
and I have not seen him since that night.

Stewart was still talking. "She came up close
and started kissing me and playing around and
rubbing against me, and I tried to make her stop,
but she said—"

"You shut up, too," I said. "You shut your
goddamn mouth and don't open it again. Not once."
I must have looked at him pretty hard then, for all
of a sudden he collapsed completely and started to
blubber.

Lucy looked at him in a sort of horror in which
there was no pity, and in that instant, when that
look flashed across her face, I knew what I was
going to do to her. I had it all straight in my mind
what I would do to her and what I had already
decided I would do to him, and there wasn't
anything left but to do it.

"All right," I said. "This is what I'm going to do.
I listened to the both of you. I listened to you all I
needed to. And now you're both going to listen to
me."

Stewart's blubbering stopped. His head came
up, the lips open and the eyes wide, staring at me.
His hands, behind him, moved nervously against
the wall. Lucy almost stopped breathing. She was
entirely off the bed now, standing on the little
white rug beside it, her long legs together, slightly

bent, and her body shrunken, her arms across her breasts, as if she were trying to cover what she no longer had to hide.

I took a step backward and sat easily in the bedroom chair she had covered in splashy chintz and I let the gun rest on my knee, my fingers loose on its butt. I looked at them steadily, from one to the other. Outside, the rain had slackened off to a rolling murmur.

"I'm going to shoot you," I said to Stewart, "right where you did it to her. I'm going to put a bullet right there, and if it doesn't kill you right away, I don't care. Because in the war, I saw a man get it there. Did you ever see that, Dick? I did and I remember about it, so that's what I'm going to do to you. If you die, good. And if you don't, they won't ever be able to suspect you of something like this again. Not ever. Not the way I'll do it, they won't."

He seemed to have turned to stone as he listened. No muscle moved in his face, as his mind refused to credit the things brought to it by his ears. And then I saw some of the fear go out of him. I knew it was because the easiest thing to be afraid of is the unknown. He knew, now; he had heard what I intended to do, it was no longer the unknown, and some of the fear left him at the knowledge. Not all of it, and none of the horror. But even for him it was better just to know.

I felt my lips slide back from my teeth again and I cocked my eyes toward Lucy.

"Either way," I said, "they won't do a thing to me. Not to Harry London, not in this county, nor for finding him in bed with my wife and shooting him. They'll turn me loose in fifteen minutes."

"Harry, please listen to me. I love you, Harry, only you, I—"

"I told you to shut up," I said. "I don't want your lies or anything else. I just want you to shut your filthy mouth. Because I'm not going to kill you. Not now or ever. Not directly. But you're going to live with me, in this house, for. the rest of your life, knowing it and remembering it. Knowing and remembering that I and everyone else also know and remember it, and worst of all"—my teeth clenched on the words—"worst of all, you're going to know and remember till the day you die what he looked like and what he was, not when he had you, but after he had you and after I shot him. Every time you come in this room or get in that bed or lay your eyes on me, you're going to remember that. I'm not going to kill you, Lucy. I'm going to do worse. I'm going to make you live with this the rest of your life. And I hope you live a long time."

Maybe it was the cold rage in my eyes or the blunt words. Maybe it was the cringing Stewart. Or maybe, for her too, it was just knowing, at last, what I was going to do. Maybe it was something else I couldn't know about. But something returned to her then, something pulled her head up and straightened her shoulders and flashed in her face, and she came across the floor and stood in front of me and bent and put her hands on my knees.

"I can't undo it, Harry," she said. "It can't be undone now, no matter what I say, no matter what I do. All right, Harry, do what you want with me. But don't add to it, Harry. Don't kill him."

It was not a plea for him. Her face and her hands and her voice told me that. Something happened to me, too, something crawled up in me and sprang the deep, unthought-of question I had shoved to the far places of my mind, the question I had not asked her and could not ask myself.

"Lucy," I whispered, "why? Why'd you do it, Lucy?"

Her eyes were deep in mine and I took my hand off the gun and touched her face, bent near mine, and for the first time I was no longer aware of her nakedness and her guilty breasts. I waited for her answer with raw hurt carved inside of me.

And in that instant, that short moment of pain, he flung himself across the room from behind her, almost flatly through space in a swimmer's racing dive. My hand closed again over the gun, but the hurtling shock of him struck against her, and she came down on me and I went over backward in the chair, Lucy on top of me, her stomach pressing into my face. At once, not only all the rage and the hate surged back inside of me, but also a flash of fear.

I struggled wildly and felt a great weight on me and then a shattering in my head. From far away came an evil roar. Then I swirled away to blackness, deep and hot and lonely.

Chapter Six

When it was light for me again that night, I lay there drowsing, with the softness of the rain still on the roof and against the panes. I was glad, I can remember how the joy burst inside of me, knowing it had all been a dream, a nebulous quirk in some dark corner of the brain, and how gratefully I began to squirm deeper into the warmth of what seemed to be the deepest, warmest mattress in the world.

And then my head ground harshly against some unyielding thing, and I started in surprise and opened my eyes, and simultaneously became aware of my skull against the hard mahogany leg of the dresser and my cheek grinding into the soft fuzz of the white rug, the popping, searing fire behind my eyelids and the parched lining of my mouth.

And in that same moment, with pure horror lurking near, waiting to pounce, I knew too, with inarguable certainty, that it had not, after all, been a dream.

Then, with succeeding shocks like the pounding of breakers against the shore, I felt the inert weight across my stomach and my right leg, touched the soft tangle that could only be hair, and looked along the floor, and saw the limp, nude leg attached to the white flank, the leg somehow flaccid and unreal, not flesh but merely old composition of some lifeless, bloodless substance.

Lucy lay across me like that and I thrust my right arm under me and pushed up with it and my left elbow and looked down at her. She was face down, the blonde head almost under my left arm, the hands on either side of the body, the legs and useless feet sprawled lifelessly. I could not see any blood, but I did not need to. The living do not lie like the dead.

The undertow of horror, of terror, of pure panic, of shock and disbelief and incomprehension grasped at my intestines, convulsive and powerful. I cried out and pushed the body away from me and dragged my legs from under it, and shoved myself back against the wall, away from it, and sat there and looked at it.

Only then did I realize I was holding the pistol.

The head had flopped toward me, the long hair tangled about it, the eyes wide open, a small trickle of blood coming from one nostril, drying in a brownish stain upon the skin. The bullet hole was above the right eye, almost but not quite even with the nose, and its evil gape was not so horrible as the slack, open mouth.

After a while, slowly, like the simmering down of boiling water when the fire is removed, repulsion for the inertness there on the white rug in front of me began to go away, and with no thought of how it had come to be there, I began to remember the times and things between us, and grief clawed at me.

This was Lucy, all there was of her. This was all of the sweetness and the glory, this was how it had ended, what it had brought her to. This was the woman I had brought to my father's house and this, ultimately, was what I had brought her to. Death, naked, ugly, and without gentleness.

"Lucy," I said, out loud, "Lucy, I'm sorry."

The emptiness of words mocked me and I drew further back to the wall. I felt the hardness of it at the back of my head and the sudden ache in my temples. And with a roar like exploding dynamite, my brain crackled with awareness of how she came to be heaped there, and of him who should be in her place.

The sonofabitch, I thought, the words almost an irreverence before the dull eyes and open mouth. And then I realized he was gone.

The rain was falling hard again, the obliterating, ceaseless rain, and I wished to be in it, to be in the rain, to let it wash it all away, clean away, to wherever the rain goes after it meets the

earth. But still I did not move from the wall and
still I could not bring myself to touch her, to close
the eyes or mouth, to bring some faint semblance
of order and decency to unordered indecent death.

So he was gone. So he had left us there, Lucy
and me, the way we had started. No, I thought, not
quite like that. Not quite the same.

But he was gone. And I was still there. And
Lucy. And something else, too, all about me in the
disordered, death-quiet room, lurking in the air,
behind the overturned chair. Something else was
there and what it was had to be discovered.

And so, at last, without bitterness, I began to
think.

The fact stared me in the face. Dick Stewart
was gone. I was alone with my dead wife. This,
somehow, was connected with the aura all about
me in that room. The link was there, but it was
vague, mist-washed, and somehow just beyond
reach.

My head was pounding steadily now, and slowly
I put the gun down and placed my hands flat on the
floor and pushed myself to my feet. I stepped
carefully around it and slowly moved across the
room to the bathroom.

My face, in the medicine-cabinet mirror, was
unchanged. Look at you, I thought—betrayed,
slugged, your wife dead. And not even a wrinkle on
your face that wasn't there before. How can so
much happen so quickly and leave no mark? Deep-
set eyes, bloodshot above a broad, blunt nose,
stared back at me from the mirror.

I knew he must have hit me with something, for
my exploring fingers found a small lump high on
the side of my head. The skin was not broken. I
washed my face in cold water. Using my two hands
for a cup, I gulped mouthfuls of it down my dry,
evil-tasting throat.

And then, in the first clarity of the clean, sweet
water, cool against my face and in my mouth, it hit

me. I straightened up and looked in the mirror again and consternation stared back at me.

Without drying my face or hands I wheeled around and stepped quickly back into the bedroom. Nothing had changed. It still lay there inert, the overturned chair beside it no more lifeless than she. Rain whispered at the windows.

Stewart's clothes were gone too. The rumpled bed jeered at me. The gun lay where I had left it. One bed-lamp burned brightly on a small table and shadows were soft on the walls.

No. Nothing had changed. Nothing, except that the invisible atmosphere in the room was no longer the scent of the unknown. It was now the smell of danger. For Dick Stewart was gone and I knew there was no trace of him remaining. The rain would have removed his footprints from the earth. It was as if he had never been there.

And I was alone with Lucy. I was alone with the gun that had killed her—my gun. My finger must have performed the physical act that had pulled its trigger. Her body lay in our bedroom. I had returned unexpectedly from a fishing trip plenty of people knew I was planning. And my reputation for violent temper had been well known since the first day I entered grade school.

There was danger in that room, all right. Danger of a jury of twelve and bars of iron and the electric chair. Danger of all that for me.

I glanced at the clock. It was eleven-thirty. It had been maybe a little after ten when I had returned. The hands of the clock told me time was short.

I sat down on the bed and my brain began to accept and reject, almost automatically. I hardly gave a thought to telling the truth, as it had happened, as much of it as I knew. I could never make it stick. Stewart would be even now sealing up an alibi with the credit-bound Negroes who traded at his general store. The room showed no trace of his having been there.

No. Even with his reputation, it would never stick.

All right, I thought, so I get the chair. So all right. I did pull that trigger, didn't I? It's what you get for murder, isn't it?

And every fiber in me sang into protest. No, by God, I thought. Goddamnit, no! I will not go to the chair for this, no matter who pulled the trigger. As sure as she lies there, that sonofabitch is responsible. She's dead because of him. And he's the one who's got to pay out for it. He's the one who's going to pay.

I would have to make him pay it out. But I couldn't do that in jail. You couldn't do anything in jail, or after they strapped you in the chair. I had to get out of it, too. I had to get clean and then there would be all of my life to make the bastard pay and pay and pay.

I looked at it again, at the long, slim legs. The substance of them had lost all beauty, even all ugliness, and merely sprawled. But I could close my eyes and conjure them up, and the rest of her, the way they had been. I could remember the long nights and the hot fires bright in us, and the hands, moving then, the legs violent and seeking, the breasts against me, soft and round and big, and the moist lips I had thought were only mine.

I could remember that and, remembering, I could hate, hate with a rage that burst from some dark recess inside me, hate for the man who had killed all that, not only killed it but taken it from me before the act of killing. I could hate for that, and maybe a little bit just for Lucy's sake, who no longer could hate or love or laugh or cry or anything, only sprawl inert upon the patient floor.

And something else, too. Something else was in me, and I looked at it and examined it and knew it for what it was. My wife had been taken in my own bed by a man about whom I had often joked, in company with others, a man whose eyes and hands coveted all women and possessed many.

And I knew I was not enough of a man, I didn't have the guts to face what I would get if I told it, to hear the quick, muffled snickers, to see the eyes, amusement veiled only a little in them, the hush of voices when you entered and they were talking, the insistent whispers. I knew it would be that way. I had seen it before, I had been a part of it. If I told it I knew it would be that way.

So, even if I could have made it stick, I knew that I would never tell the truth of what had happened in that room that night. Had I killed him, the county would have respected that, sympathized with it. But he had got away, and I didn't have what it took to face it.

So I had to be free of it too. Then there would be just the two of us, and a way could be found. A way could always be found.

I got up and went across the room. I closed my eyes and leaned over and put my hands beneath the arms. Already, it seemed to me, the clay chill was on the flesh.

I dragged it, limp and sprawling, across the room and put my leg behind the dressing-table chair and let it down into it. At first it kept slumping forward, and then I gritted my teeth and put my hand under the chin and tipped the head back. Sightless eyes fixed on the ceiling. The arms dangled loosely on either side of the chair, but it stayed upright and I moved away.

The robe lay on the floor where I had flung it. I picked it up and brushed it carefully...The reminiscence of her clung to it. I folded it across my arm, carefully, and went slowly back to the dressing table.

It was hard to get the arms into it, but I managed. I had to manage. More than once my hand brushed across the breasts, each time shock coming at me that I should touch them without the answering rush in my veins. I pulled the robe closely about it, finally, and put it back into the chair and tipped the head back again. The arms still dangled.

I looked at it carefully. There could be no other chance if I fouled it up now. The bullet had entered the forehead above the right eye, angling toward the center of the head, and powder stains smoked the edges of the dark wound. That was the only blessing I could see in the whole business. It could make no difference to her now if the gun had been one foot or twenty feet away.

Again I slowly crossed the room. I picked up the gun and took out my handkerchief and spent a good five minutes patiently wiping prints from its surface. Then I trudged the long distance back to the dressing table, carrying the gun in my handkerchief.

I took the limp right hand in mine and closed it about the butt. The hand was small and the index finger barely spanned the distance to the trigger.

I raised the hand, still clutched on the pistol, until the barrel pointed exactly into the wound a few inches away. Then I let the hand fall and the gun clattered on the floor.

You're good, I thought. Boy, you're good. For an amateur you're doing all right. You ought to be a pro.

So that was that and I only had to touch it once more. I got another handkerchief from the dresser and, wearily now, I walked out of the bedroom and into the hall and on down it toward the dark living room. I went over to the desk from which I had taken the gun.

Her portable was there, the battered old Underwood she had brought with her and used for the voluminous correspondence she had carried on with old friends. With a handkerchief in each hand, I picked it up, careful not to touch it, and carried it back to the bedroom.

I returned again to the living room and opened a drawer and, again with a handkerchief, picked up a sheet of typing paper. I went back to the bedroom and rolled the paper into the machine.

Still using the two handkerchiefs, I picked the typewriter up again and carried it over and put it down in the lap. I squatted at the left side and steadied the machine on the sprawled legs with my left hand. I reached across it with my right and took the right arm and pulled it into its lap. Then I took the right index finger in my hand.

The slow, solemn tap-tap-tap was ominous in the stillness of the room. I felt profuse sweat on my brow and my head was aching badly now. But I kept on punching the lifeless finger at the keyboard until I had spelled out, all in capital letters:

HARRY IS UNFAITHFUL.

I JUST CAN'T TAKE IT.

I let the right hand fall back to its side and I took the two handkerchiefs again and picked up the portable and put it on her dressing table. That was all right because she used it in here often, as well as at the living-room desk.

I put one of the handkerchiefs in my pocket and carried the other one to the bathroom and dropped it in the clothes hamper. And then it was done.

But there was still time. I had to be sure. One mistake was all it would take. One mistake could fry me in that evil little armchair up at State Prison. One mistake and Dick Stewart would go free forever.

I sat down on the bed and put my elbows on my knees and my chin in my hands. I studied the whole thing out, the way it was, and the way it would look to them. I turned it in my mind and I started right from the beginning and went through it to the end and tried to see the loose ends dangling. My aching head didn't make it any easier. But I forced myself to think it through.

It's a good thing I did. Because I had made two mistakes. Two glaring boners. Maybe more, too, but I couldn't find them, and just the two were bad enough.

The first would be easy to fix. I had wiped the gun absolutely clean of fingerprints and had put hers on it. It didn't stand to reason that my prints wouldn't also be on my own pistol, a souvenir I had lugged back with me from Italy. So that had to be done all over.

I sat there, staring at the second mistake. It was on the white rug, a little brown stain of blood I hadn't even seen until now, ten feet away from where I had placed the body. I could drag the body back over there to the blood, but it wouldn't look as good, as real as I had made it.

I thought about it until the way came to me. It came to me how I could fix it up about the blood and at the same time seal the case up tight, remove any doubt there might be in their minds when they came.

I got up and got the handkerchief out of the hamper and went back over to the dressing table and picked up the typewriter and put it in the lap again, and held it the same as before. And then I took the finger and punched out another line, beneath the first one:

NOW WE'LL BE TOGETHER FOREVER.

I put the typewriter back on the dressing table. I stood up, walked around the chair, and picked up the gun. I went back to the bathroom and dropped the handkerchief back in the hamper. I came back into the bedroom and, with the other handkerchief, wiped the gun.

I handled it, carelessly, all over, clicking the safety on and off, touching the barrel, just the way you might handle any gun if it was yours and you were used to it.

Then I went over and stood by the blood spot on the rug and held the gun in my right hand, at arm's length, and pointed it back toward my left arm. I took a full minute getting the aim just as it had to be.

Gently, I squeezed the trigger.

Chapter Seven

I caught one in the war, too, so the shock of it slamming into the muscle of my arm didn't surprise me, or the force with which I spun half around.

But no matter how often you've been hit, the pain is just as bad. It was just as bad then, maybe worse, and I reeled and funny lights came on in my head. The gun fell out of my hand and I dropped on my knees to the rug.

There was plenty of blood and I slowly stretched out and let it run and cover up the little brown spot on the rug. I began to feel better lying there. I was warm and the pain began to go away and I wanted to lie there forever and just let it all go, and never get up.

But I watched the blood, pumping regularly from the upper part of my arm, and knew I had to get up. Using my good arm, I pushed myself to my knees and staggered up. I stood there swaying and the pain was back. I reached over and pulled the edges of cloth away from the wound and bit my lip sharply. I steadied myself.

I tore the sleeve off, at the shoulder seam, with one hard jerk. I wrapped it around my arm, tightly, and the blood flow began to slow up. I stood there and tried to think. There was something else, something final that had to be done.

Then I remembered the gun and that was it. Slowly, I went down on one knee and picked it up. I had to stay down there and breathe a minute before I could get back up.

But finally I made it and then I lurched across that wide room and knelt once more by the body. The blood dripped behind me, but I didn't care.

Let it drip, I thought. Let it run all over the floor.

This time I didn't have the strength to raise the arm. But I got the gun in the hand, somehow, and pressed the stiffening fingers around it and let it fall.

Now, goddamnit, I thought. It's done. It's finished.

I went back across the room and out into the hall again and staggered on back to the kitchen. I smeared blood all over the clean white cabinets, but at last I got the bottle down from an upper shelf and pulled the cork out with my teeth and took a long, long drink. It exploded in my stomach, and when I went back into the hall, I was stronger, if not steadier.

I picked up the phone from the little desk just beyond the bedroom door. I got the county operator and when I said, "Sheriff's office," she plugged the call right in for me.

It rang twice before a sleepy voice answered.

"Walt?"

"He ain't here. Depity James talkin'."

"Bill. Bill James."

"Yeah. Who's this?"

"Bill, you get Walt. I don't care where he is. Get him and get out to my place."

"Who is this?"

"Harry London."

"Oh, yeah. What's the trouble, Harry?"

"Never mind. Just get Walt and get out here."

"I don't know, Harry, he said—"

"Get him," I said. "My wife just killed herself."

When they came up on the porch, the rain had stopped completely. I was sitting on the floor in the bedroom, against the opposite wall from the dressing table. The bottle was beside me on the floor and it was almost empty now.

I called out to them and they came on back to the lighted bedroom door and stopped there and looked around at the blood-splattered room.

Walt's deep-set eyes lighted on the bottle.

"Good," he said. "Ease off the shock."

"Go to hell," I said.

"Take it easy, Harry."

He went over to the dressing table and touched it once and then he leaned over and read the note. He looked quickly at me and this time saw the arm and the tourniquet. He came quickly across the room and knelt by me and looked at the wound.

"You, Bill," he said. "Go git that first-aid stuff in the car and then drive Harry to the hospital."

Bill faded out of the door.

Walt rocked back on his lean haunches.

"All this blood your'n?"

"It's ketchup. Don't you know ketchup from blood?"

He looked at the bottle again and moved it from my reach.

"You got the shock eased off enough," he said. "Tell me about it."

I closed my eyes and let my head go back against the wall.

"I came back from that fishing trip I planned. Stormed on me and I came back. She wasn't expecting me and I came in quiet. Going to surprise her."

I heard Bill come back up on the porch.

"She was sitting there where she is now. She had the gun. First thing I saw when I opened the door. 'What the hell,' I said. She didn't say anything. She just got up and came over, and stood right in front of me, holding the gun. 'Put that thing down,' I told her."

Bill put the first-aid kit in Walt's hand. Walt opened it and began to fumble around inside of it.

"Then she said, 'You're back,' just like that, in a funny kind of voice. 'Yeah,' I said, and I started to reach out and get the gun and then she said, 'that makes it better.' And then she lifted up the gun and pointed it at me and I hollered and she shot me before I could move."

"Take it easy," Walt said again. He shook a powder out over the wound and began to fish in the kit for gauze.

"I went down. I couldn't even move. I guess she thought I was dead. I tried to holler or something but I couldn't make a sound. It was like I was paralyzed. And then I heard that typewriter going and I knew I was crazy. It must be a dream, I thought. And about that time the typing stopped and in a minute the gun went off again."

He was bandaging the wound now, but his eyes were on mine. I managed to keep staring at him and I thought the whisky was good protection. If I acted funny they could blame it on that.

"I had to just lay there but pretty soon I got to where I could move and then I got up and crawled over there and saw what it was. After a while I got this tourniquet and went back and got the bottle and called you."

You can't prove it a goddamn bit different, I thought, not if you wanted to. A hick sheriff like you, spending half your time with those roosters you're always fighting. Just get it over with, that's all.

For God's sake, just get it over with.

The bandage was finished and he nodded at Bill. Bill helped me up and I grabbed the bottle again and killed it in one swallow and threw it on the bed. That's where you belong, I thought. In the bed with the other dead soldiers.

"Bill will take you to the hospital," Walt was saying. "I'll handle ev'rything here. Then you get some sleep an' we'll talk tomorrow."

"Tomorrow's a big word," I said.

"It'll get here."

So I let Bill take my arm and help me and we were almost out of that room when Walt spoke again.

"That note, Harry. What it says right?"

I looked at him a long time. So what? I thought. What difference does it make now?

"Hell," I said, "you never knew a guy to turn it down when it came along, did you?"

He pursed his lips.

"Some," he said. "One or two."

"Go to hell," I said, and we went on out into the hall.

And, like death, the thing I had forgotten came at me out of the dark.

My hands.

I hadn't washed them. Not since firing the shot into my arm.

Did Walt know about paraffin tests? The only thing he knew about police work was how to handle a gun. But he could have learned about that test like I had, reading Dick Tracy. And if he got suspicious … I swore to myself as we came out on the porch. The rain had stopped, but the night smelled of it and the air was cool. The moon was out now and it glinted on a puddle in front of the steps.

We started down the steps and I let a foot drag and pitched forward. My good arm slipped through Bill's fingers and I went face down in the puddle, both arms in front of me.

The pain was, for a moment, more than I could bear, and I could almost feel the tremendous surge of the blood again. But my hands were deep in the puddle and I ground them into the mud and covered them over the wrists with the rain water and let them stay there.

Bill quickly helped me up then and we looked at the blood, pumping regularly again.

"I better get Walt to fix that," he said.

"The hell with Walt." I started toward the car.

He hesitated, then came after me.

It was a long ride to town, but no longer than my thoughts, and the shooting, slashing pains in my arm and shoulder hurt no more than the nails someone slowly drove into my sides.

Lucy, I thought.

Lucy.
Why did you do it?

They held a coroner's inquest, but that's as far as it went.

Ours is a pretty backwoods county. It looked like suicide and I had said it was suicide, so as far as they were concerned it was suicide.

It wasn't as if any of them had really known Lucy well, grown up and gone to school with her. It wasn't even as if the ones of them who had known her at all even liked her very much. Lucy had had New York City written all over her, and in Coshocken County, where the county seat town of St. Johns has a population of less than a thousand, that went over like a polecat at a picnic.

The clothes she ordered from New York stores, the way she walked and wore her hair and talked and laughed ... the county never got used to any of those things. So when everything pointed to her having killed herself, trying to include me in the deal, the coroner's jury and everyone else chalked it up to the fact that she was a Yankee and a mighty queer piece to boot.

After it all happened, I began to feel that somehow in this fact lay the key to what Lucy had done. I had known she was lonely on the farm, far away from friends and familiar places, but there had been no outward indications of boredom or strain.

We'd been married in New York, just before I went overseas as an engineer captain. When I came back, nearly two years later, I was a major and the war was over and Coshocken County looked, from New York's gay spots, like the hind end of hell. So I kept the oak leaves on for a while, and Lucy and I had a spell of Army life on the West Coast.

We had a high old time, what with my pay and the big postwar profits from the farm my father had left me, and which Brax Jordan, my lawyer,

was operating for me. But it palled on me
gradually, and one day when I suggested I resign
and we try Coshocken for a while, she said all right,
without eagerness but seemingly without regret.

We had been there a little less than a year the
night I came home to find her in bed with Dick
Stewart. Somewhere in that year, the boredom and
the quiet and the loneliness must have become too
much for the city-bred girl. Only she hadn't told me
about it, and maybe that was because I had settled
back into the old life as if I had never been away,
as if I would stay there forever. Which I would
have. Only not if I had known. Not then. I was a
trained engineer. We could have gone anywhere,
and no farm, no way of life in the world, would have
been worth losing her.

So there had been, I figured, the loneliness and
the boredom and then there had been Dick
Stewart. He has a big store in St. Johns, only it
isn't his. It belongs to his wife, a polio victim who
won't ever walk again, and he married her to get it.
But a store and plenty of tobacco money isn't
enough for him.

He has to have women. Sometimes he'll get you
aside and tell you about his trips to the state
capital and the girls he has there and what he does
with them and you can see it in his eyes, the way
he has to have them. Only the trips have to be
infrequent and there have to be women in between
and there are.

And there isn't a soul in the county who would
be surprised to hear that Dick Stewart had been
shot in someone else's bedroom or barn loft, and
there are plenty of them who'll tell you there's more
than one youngster around named Brigman or
Meakins or Buxton or Bailey, with the same blue
eyes and curly hair and dark skin Dick Stewart
has.

So there must have been the loneliness and the
boredom for her, then Stewart. Finally there was

the bedroom and the fear, the blood on the white rug and the inert sprawl of the legs and the sightless glass of the eyes.

But it had all come out the way I had planned, and nobody, as far as I knew, even had an idea it wasn't suicide. Except Dick Stewart. And he, I was sure, was keeping his mouth shut, because of that rich, paralytic wife who held his purse strings. Because he couldn't afford not to keep quiet; he had nothing to gain and everything to lose if he didn't keep his mouth shut.

And now I could deal with him in my own way, at my own leisure. There was plenty of time, and I intended to use it. I would make him pay out for Lucy and for me. I would make him pay out, all right. But when I did, it would be foolproof. When I did, it would be like it had been with Lucy. It would look the way I wanted it to look.

There was plenty of time to figure it out, to figure how to do it, and, sweetest of all, every day I delayed was one more day through which he would have to live, waiting for it, knowing it was coming, knowing it had to come, but not when, not how, not where.

That was the sweetest of all, to know it was going to be like that for him until the day I decided to end it, to know the terror and the despair and the incomparable aloneness of him waiting for me to do it, somewhere, sometime, somehow.

I began to plan murders. I planned them cold-bloodedly and deliberately, without a qualm of conscience in me, only black merciless hate, because he had it coming to him. I had the power and the right to do it. Without guilt, I planned murder upon murder, and then discarded each plan because there was a flaw, a catch, a weak link that couldn't be trusted. And then I planned again.

I had plenty of time, you see. One thing had gone wrong. Three days after Lucy's death, the surgeon had amputated my left arm just below the shoulder, had left this ugly, reminding stump, this dangling, freakish monument to all I owed to Dick Stewart.

Chapter Eight

It was amazing how simply a whole life could be ended.

I don't mean just the mortality that had been Lucy's, but the whole of a life together that had been built between us. For her part, she had had no family, except a distant aunt and uncle who kept discreetly silent about the whole thing, after I had Brax Jordan notify them.

As simply as that, with only the additional complication of a funeral I could not attend, and which few others cared to attend, and the meaningless purchase of a tombstone, she went to dust and memory.

As for the rest of it, as soon as I was on the road to recovery from my arm operation I called in Jordan again. His quick lawyer's eyes narrowed when I told him what I wanted.

"Don't be a fool, Harry!"

"And then," I said, "you take what you get for it and settle up my debts and buy me the old Caldwell place."

He shook his head.

"They must have you doped up."

"Look, Brax. You just do what I say. Let the bright remarks go."

He chewed furiously at his cigar. It was nearly as big as he was. Brax Jordan was a little fellow, not much over five-four. His head, set solidly on amazingly wide shoulders, seemed far too big for his body.

Maybe that head was just bulging with brain. A lot of people thought so, anyway. He had smashed all records at law school, and when he finished he could have had his pick of jobs with any number of big-city law firms. Yet he had come back to St. Johns to open his own practice.

Oddly enough, it had made him rich, because he combined his law work with some of the shrewdest farm real estate deals the county had ever seen. His holdings were far bigger than mine, although he owned no single piece of land as big as the London place.

His father and my father had been friends, and in the same way, Brax and I were friends too. It was more than an acquaintance growing out of business relations. He and I had hunted together and fished together and grown up together. When the other kids had ragged him about his size, I had used my own big body to shut them up.

He had paid that debt back, years later, by doing his best to make the county accept Lucy, although he had never been able to force her down their throats.

He took the cigar out of his mouth and looked at me, the big head shaking slightly from side to side.

"Harry, you and I have been friends a mighty long time. Now I'm a lawyer and I take that seriously. Mighty seriously. And you own the best and biggest farm in this part of the state. As a lawyer and even more as your friend, I can't let you sell that farm for the peanuts it'll bring compared to what it's worth. And even if I could, I'll be damned if I'd turn around and buy that damn desert with the money."

"All right. I'll get Murdoch Smith to handle it."

He snorted. "He'd skin your eyebrows. Harry, you have to snap out of this."

"Out of what?"

"Whatever it is. There's no sense in any of it. So Lucy got crazy ideas in her head. So you're all cut up. That's understandable. But for the Lord's sake, man, you can't chuck everything for the rest of your life!"

"I don't aim to."

"Then what the hell do you want with the Caldwell place? There's not a building on it. It won't even grow sandspurs."

"The hell with it, Brax. You want to handle it?"

He got up and went over to the window and flipped the cigar out.

"No. Get yourself another boy."

"All right. You mind calling Smith to come over?"

He looked at me steadily.

"Goddamn your eyes," he said. "Goddamn Smith, too. I'll get to work on it."

"Good. Anything you get over what it costs for the Caldwell place and maybe a thousand dollars, fix it up for ..." I thought a minute. "For the polio foundation."

Brax shook his head from side to side, slowly. His mouth was slightly open.

"Close your mouth," I said. "I'll tell you once and that's all. That farm is what did this to me and Lucy. That and—something else. I don't want to see the place again, or hear about it, or have money from it, or any goddamn thing at all. I don't want to even think about it. Now—you see?"

"Maybe. But now about the something else?"

"I'll fix the something else, too. Sometime."

He looked at me shrewdly.

"I never would have thought it," he said. "Old Puritan Harry London. The guy who could preach whole sermons about the sanctity of the home. Harry, just how and when were you, of all people, unfaithful to Lucy?"

That was too close, I thought. Way too close. I changed the subject, wincing as if he had touched upon a tender nerve.

"One other thing, Brax. There's an old trunk out there in the attic. Get it down and put some of my clothes in it, whatever you think I might need, and that picture of my folks and some blankets and stuff like that."

"How about Lucy's things?"

"That goes with the sale. All of it."

"Do you think that will do any good? Do you think that will get her out of your mind?"

"I don't know. I just don't want any of her stuff around."

"By the way," he said. "The sheriff sent the pistol over to my office. Said to give it back to you when you were up again. You don't want it, do you?"

"Yes," I said. "Put that in the trunk too."

Brax sold the place for me and then bought the Caldwell place. He put the thousand I had decided to hold out in the bank for me, plus enough to cover my hospital bills, and fixed up the rest for the polio foundation.

When I got out of the hospital, I went to the bank and got the money in small bills. I went to Brax and got the trunk from him and asked him if he'd drive me out to the Caldwell place.

He got out his car and we drove uptown and I went into the hardware store and bought a rifle, some cartridges, and a tool kit. They sold building supplies, too, and I ordered some lumber and a Cadet heater and a length of stovepipe. Then I went to the dime store and bought two or three cheap dishes, some ten-cent silverware, a frying pan, and a coffeepot.

I went back to the car and asked Brax to drive down Hertford Street, and sure enough, there were plenty of them there. I motioned Brax to stop and stuck my head out the window.

"You, boy," I said. "You want to work a day or two?"

The colored man shuffled closer to the car. Huge muscles rippled in his arms.

"Doin' what, Cap'n?"

"Building a shack."

He considered this.

"Fifty cents an hour?"

"I'll give you five dollars a day till we finish."

The broad face squeezed into thought, ponderously balancing off fifty cents an hour against five dollars a day.

"I reck'n so, Cap'n."

He got in the back seat and we drove out of town. About a mile out, I told Brax to stop again and I went into a filling station and bought bacon and coffee, a dozen cans of beans, some corn meal and canned milk. Then we went on again.

We turned off the paved highway and followed a bumpy clay road about five miles. A rutted road led off to the left through scraggly brush. Brax slowed for the turn.

"We'll get out here," I said.

He stopped the car and the Negro and I got out and took the stuff out of the car. The hardware-store truck wouldn't be more than a mile or two behind, I figured.

Brax sat there staring at me.

"Thanks for everything," I said. "See you sometime."

He pulled out a cigar, in his lawyer's way of taking plenty of time about what he had to say.

"All this"—he held a match to the cigar—"doesn't impress me very much."

"It's not meant to."

"But it is. You want us—the county—to know you're hurt. You want us to feel sorry for you. You want us to say, 'Poor old Harry, living out there all alone because of what that Yankee girl did to him'."

I laughed. The Negro moved uneasily.

"Well, I'm not sorry for you. You're a damn fool, Harry. Why don't you use your head?"

"Why don't you go back to town?"

He shrugged and let in the clutch. He turned the car around in the narrow road and the Negro and I watched him head back the way we had come.

I sat down under a tree and the Negro squatted nearby, his eyes nervous and his face carefully expressionless.

"Got to wait for a truck," I said.

Pretty soon it came along, rattly and slow, dust clouding behind it. It slowed down and made the turn and then the colored driver saw us and stopped. The Negro and I climbed into the back with the lumber and the stove.

"Just a little way now," I told the driver.

The truck shackled on through the scrub, and in a minute or two the bushes and small trees fell behind us. It's seventy miles from the sea, but the sea may have covered it once, for all I know. Those dunes, they shift sometimes in the wind. This sand won't grow anything at all. A man named Caldwell once thought oil lay under this geological freak of sand and hard white clay and scattered bunches of bladelike grass. So he bought it all and built a shack and a rickety derrick and went to drilling.

He never struck anything, but after he died geologists came to make sure the old man wasn't just crazy, thinking there was oil under here. He may not have been crazy, but all the geologists found were old sea shells and the shifting, biding sand.

And now it's mine. That day, we went on along the almost disappearing road and then we saw green again, the few sparse trees around that inexplicable spring of cool, sweet water. The four canted posts of the old derrick, it's superstructure gone with the years, were stark against the sky. Old Man Caldwell's cabin had long ago disappeared.

"All right," I said to the driver. "Stop here."

The driver and the Negro unloaded the truck and I paid the driver. He got in the truck, turned it around, and went back the way he had come, the truck moving more swiftly now.

I went over by the spring and I looked around a minute and then I took a stick and drew a ten-foot square in the soft earth.

"We'll build here, boy."

"O.K., Cap'n."

The rest of that day we worked and then we rolled into blankets from the trunk and slept till the sun called us and all the next day we worked and then slept again and finished it the third day. I was of little use as yet, with only my one arm, but the Negro was a hard worker.

Then we had it finished, one room, square and unpainted, a small hole for a window, another larger one for a door, and one just large enough for the stovepipe, with a slanting shed roof and no porch. The floor was plain lumber, and we had built a bunk into one corner and some shelves along the opposite wall and a larger one against the blank rear wall for eating.

I gave him the fifteen dollars, and his thanks, except for questions asked and instructions given, were very nearly the first words between us since the car had stopped on Hertford Street. He took a few steps along the road away from me and then he stopped and looked back.

"You aim to live here, Cap'n?"

"Yes."

He shook his head. "Don't laugh at me, now, Cap'n, but there's sperrits here."

"What spirits?"

"Just sperrits. I heard 'em last night. Bad, Cap'n. This ain't no place to live."

Anger flared in me as if a sudden storm had crashed in my stomach.

"Get your black carcass off my land," I said.

He turned around and walked off up the road, not hurrying, just plodding steadily away from there. I went back and sat down in the door of the cabin and looked at where my arm had been and swore out loud.

But after a while the fury went out of me and I began to make plans again. An idea came to me and I thought about it, examining it carefully until dark, and then I found the flaw in it and discarded the idea and went on into the shack and got a can of beans off the shelf and hacked it open with the ax.

Chapter Nine

But the Negro was right. Maybe there aren't any spirits. Maybe he just felt something in the air, the atmosphere. But whatever it was, he was right about it.

Because something happened to my brain out there. Maybe I was a little crazy with it, the hate and the longing and the sorrow and the dark, nameless voice in me ceaselessly asking, *Why?* Maybe it was the loneliness and the eternal sand, or the never ending beans and bacon, or the silence at night. Maybe it was all of that.

But whatever it was, whether it was crazy or not, some giant grip took hold of my brain and steadily squeezed on it until it stopped. I could no longer, literally, think. My body moved and functioned. Some instinct supplied what it had to have, the motions, the food, the rest, or rather the stretching of bones and flesh upon the unyielding bunk.

But beyond that, cells and lobes refused to go. The careful calculation of the hospital days was impossible now. I could not even remember what those exhaustive, always flawed plans had been, much less conceive new ones. The ability to think, to reason, to apply logic was squeezed out of me, and in its place an image rose: a face, swart, handsome, always smiling, with not only mockery but defiance in the deep blue of the eyes, with tumbling curly hair, the lips moist and wet, Stewart's face, bodiless, bloodless, fleshless, always before me, always mocking, always haunting even the tortured fever of sleep.

The image persisted until it was no longer image but reality, like the spring or the four ghostly posts, the skeletons against sand and sky. It persisted until one day I took a stick six feet long and drove it into the earth about twenty yards from my door and placed an empty bean can over the end of it and went back and sat in the door until the face came, leering from what had once been a can of beans, and then I took the rifle and methodically began to put bullets through the can.

When that one was full of holes, I put up another can, and then another, and thereafter the image appeared always sieved with dark, evil holes, none of them different from the hole in Lucy's head about which the stain of exploding powder was seared.

But the plan did not come, the plan to which my days were to have been devoted, the plan to which I would someday apply my hand like an implacable god. It devolved into an ethereal face and a can of beans and a rifle, a dream that inevitably faded before the final moment of knowledge.

The hand still squeezed on me, cells and lobes still stagnated, and I remained a god without lightning.

Yes, the Negro was right. And one night, when I had been here three months, the loneliness and the hurt and the hate, the face in the can, and the impotence told me he had been right. And I walked out of the little shack and out of the road and down it to a small unpainted farmhouse set back among overbearing trees.

When I returned, I put the two fruit jars on the floor by the door, got a can of beans off the shelf, emptied them in the unwashed frying pan, and then took the can out and hung it on the stick. I went back to the shack, got the rifle from the corner, sat down in the door, and took a drink from one of the jars.

Pretty soon, in the moonlight, I could see the face in the can and I lifted the rifle and put a bullet over its right eye, a little in toward the nose. Then I put the rifle down and took another drink and waited for the face to come again.

I was drunk.

I had to lean for a moment against the candy counter, my eyes furry and my mouth a little slack, and then I had my feet firmly on the floor under me again and I walked on over to the potbellied stove, glowing red against the raw winter chill.

There was a vacant chair in the circle around it and I lurched down on it, feeling the sharp edge of the pistol in my hip pocket.

"Well, Harry," the man sitting next to me said. My eyes focused slowly on him and I saw that it was George Aitken, who owned a small farm beyond my own. Or what had been my own.

I looked at him and there couldn't have been any greeting in my eyes, because I didn't feel any inside of me. After a moment he turned his head and sent a blob of tobacco juice sizzling against the side of the stove.

I concentrated slowly on the three other men around the stove. None of them looked at me, although I had known them all most of my life. The hell with them, I thought, the hell with all of them. They didn't know. They don't know anything.

I reached into the pocket of the heavily lined hunting jacket that had been one of the things Brax Jordan had kept out for me when he sold off the farm. My hand clutched the fruit jar and brought it out. It slipped from my hand, but the heavy glass did not break on the floor.

I lunged down on one knee to pick it up and then I lost my balance and threw out my arm to catch myself, and knelt like that on the floor, my head hanging and my mouth open and my breathing heavy. I laughed, loudly and harshly, and I picked up the jar and hauled myself back into the chair.

I offered the jar vaguely around the circle.

"Have a drink," I said, my tongue leaden in my mouth. "Bes' ol' white y'ever tas'ed."

They did not look at me and nobody spoke. I was not even capable of anger any more, and I laughed again.

"'S your fun'ral," I said, and turned the jar up and drank.

And then I saw him, standing just outside the circle of silent men, his hands on his hips, looking very steadily at me. Something like a shiver ran down my spine and I was conscious again of the bulk of the pistol in my pocket. I took the jar down from my lips and leaned forward, my forearm on my knee, and looked back at him.

"Th' Grea' Lov'r," I said. "If's 'not th' Grea' Lov'r."

His lips twitched.

"If you have to drink that stuff in here, I wish you'd go back to the storeroom," he said, his voice very flat.

You ought to be afraid, my fuzzy brain thought. You ought to be shaking in your goddamn boots because I'm going to kill you, now, today, here and now and forever, I'm going to blast a hole right through you, right where I said I would, and they'll all see it, and you'll be dead, dead, dead, and it will all be finished.

And I said, "Drink where I goddamn please."

"Not in here," he said. "I don't want any law trouble."

I threw back my head and laughed loudly again. I screeched and my empty laughter howled back at me from the high ceiling of the old store building. The men did not look at me.

"A'right," I said. "No trouble, no trouble a-tall. C'mon back'n have one with me."

"I got work to do."

"Y'better c'mon," I said. "Y'better have one."

"Not now. You go on."

Suddenly it became very quiet in the long room. Nobody moved. Stewart looked steadily at me and my sodden brain forced my eyes to focus on his. I shifted my weight off the pistol and stood up, swaying, and I heard the thick words stumble from my lips.

"Y'better c'mon," I said. "Tongue goes l'il loose w'en I drink."

The eyes changed quickly, warning flashing into them.

"All right," he said. "Just for a minute."

"'Sall it'll take. Jus' a minit."

And I laughed again. I stumbled past the stove, lurching against Aitken, and he drew away from me, not quickly, and I looked at him and went on.

"S'cuse me," I said. "S'cuse hell out of me."

It was an endless walk back to the storeroom at the end of the building. The heat from the stove did not carry more than halfway back, but I did not notice the chill. I stumbled against tables and counters of goods, still holding the jar reeling through the store, and I knocked over a plow that stood on the floor; but I did not look back.

Now I'm going to do it, I thought. The hell with all of it, the hell with waiting any longer. I'm going to do it and get it over with and let them take me and then that will end too and it will be over. Everything will be over then.

The storeroom was dark and chilly and I turned around and leaned back against a pile of fertilizer bags and drank from the jar again. Then he came in and stopped just inside the door.

I held out the jar. He shook his head and his words snapped at me.

"What do you want?"

"Want? Me?"

"You got something on your mind."

"Plenny. Got plenny on my min'."

"You got to quit coming here like this. This is the fifth time now."

"S'last time. No more."

His voice was suspicious. "You want money?"

I laughed. "Maybe I'm goin' to kill you."

It was his turn to laugh, and he did, not loudly, a short bark of derision.

"You'd have done it a long time ago," he said, "if you had the guts. If you hadn't made a bum out of yourself." He spat on the floor. "And you won't get any money, either. You're in this deeper than I am. You have to keep your mouth shut too."

I set the jar down on the fertilizer bags and put my hand in my hip pocket, touching the gun. He did not seem to notice the movement.

"Get out of here," he said. "Don't come back. You had your chance the night you came through that door and you didn't do it. And you won't ever do it because you've drunk up all your guts and you're too ashamed to admit I took your wife."

I pulled out the pistol and pointed it at him. He looked at me calmly, not the way he had that night in Lucy's bedroom, and he did not laugh now, but his voice mocked me.

"No," he said, "you won't do it. Because if you did, they'd all know then, they'd all know about me and her. And you couldn't take that. You have to stay drunk just because you know it. You won't do anything to let them know too."

I stared at him and he did not move, his face calm, and I felt my finger tighten on the trigger and then my arm fell to my side.

"Maybe sometime in the back," he said. "Maybe you'll try to do it that way. But not out in the open. Not so they'll find out about it."

He was right. Even my whisky-soaked brain screamed it at me. I didn't have the guts, not just to pull that trigger, but to let it all come out. Inside of me there was still the shame and the knowledge of the triumph that this man held over me, a secret inner triumph, known only to him and to me, so that when my triumph came, if it ever did, it too had to be the same, secret and inside and known only to him and to me, so that I could tote up the scores and cross them off, and know that not only his triumph and finally mine but also the very contest itself would then not only vanish but would actually never have been.

I never hated him so much. But I knew he was right. And I knew, too, with hopeless despair, that the way would never come to me, that I was frozen, incapable, that I would neither face the consequences of shooting him openly nor conquer him with secret, obliterating death, and that I would live the rest of my life bound by it, by the chain of my own weakness and the eternal, torturing ropes of memory.

I knew all that as I lurched past him, back down the long room to the door, past the set, averted faces of the men at the stove, out into the bleak, raw afternoon, the wind cutting down the street hard now, slicing into me, but no deeper than my own thin, dying knowledge of myself.

Chapter Ten

The glow had crept in from the east while I told it to her, and when I had finished it, we sat there in the gray light, a little chilly and shivery, and we could see the edge of the sun rising crimson and stark against the morning sky.

"So that's why I'm out here all alone," I said. "That's why I'm dirty, like you said. That's why none of it really matters now. That's why I'm not going to stop you from telling."

"That's a hell of a story," she said. "And I don't believe a word of it."

"All right. I don't blame you. But I had to get it off my chest. I had to get it out of me to somebody that I killed her. And now you can go. I won't stop you."

She looked at me dully and then she got up from the running board and stretched herself in the warming sun.

"You're a good talker," she said. "I never heard anybody could talk like that before. But you're making it all up. Lucy wasn't that kind."

"I saw it. It's the truth."

"I almost wish it was. You must have been halfway decent once. You must have been quite a guy."

"I'm sorry you don't believe it. But I reckon you have your reasons."

She looked at me steadily.

"I knew her better than you ever did," she said. "And I've got a letter from her. She wrote me lots of letters. But this one says she was afraid you'd kill her if you ever found out—something."

That made me blink. I hadn't known she was afraid of me. I had a violent temper and she knew it, but I had never raised my hand to her.

"Maybe you better tell me a few things," I said. "What was she afraid I'd find out?"

"I need some coffee."

"I'm sorry," I said. "I stopped buying it. It got too expensive. Most of my money ran out a long time ago. There's just enough now for—"

"I know. Well, I couldn't stand that whisky of yours."

"We could get some coffee. That dirt road out there runs out to the highway and there's an all-night joint. It's about six miles."

"Let's go."

She drove fast, but not carelessly, and the old car careened down the dirt road toward the highway and we sat there, side by side, and I looked out the window and tried not to think at all, not even about what it could be that Lucy had been afraid I would learn.

I don't know what she thought about, or if she thought at all, but she didn't say anything either and pretty soon we turned into the highway and she picked up a little more speed. Finally, she spoke:

"Even if I could believe Lucy would play around, I can't see her going for some backwoods Romeo."

"You don't know Stewart," I said. "He's got plenty of money. He's good-looking, I give him that. And he's got the nerve to make whatever play it takes to get whoever he wants. You just don't know him."

"I'd like to. Then I'd know. I'd know if Lucy could go for him."

Then we were pulling up in front of the Eat-Rite Griddle. The garish blue neon outlining the roof of the shabby building clashed against the morning light. I had put on a shirt before we left, and my shoes, and I had turned my back while she put on a blouse in place of the torn T shirt. But we must have been a strange pair, the tall, gaunt man with the wild shock of black hair and beard and the dirty clothes, the grime of weeks on his face and hands and neck, and the trim blonde in slacks, with a purple bruise across the side of her face, both a little worn-looking in the glare of a new day.

A long-necked youth sat on a stool before the counter, reading a comic book. He looked over his shoulder at us as we entered, and his eyes widened a little at the sight of my beard and her black eye, and he rolled up the comic book and slipped it in his hip pocket and followed us to a booth, wiping his hands on a grease-grimed apron.

"You want breakfast?"

"Yes," she said. "I'm starved. What's good?"

He reached across the booth and took a torn menu from behind the napkin holder and handed it to her. She looked at it a moment and he stood there, his hands uneasy.

"I'll have Jack's Joy and coffee," she said, and handed it to me.

I looked for Jack's Joy. The menu said it was "One Golden-Fried Egg Resting Triumphantly on a Delectable Waffle. With Maple Sirup."

"My God," I said. "Bring me some ham and two eggs over light."

Her face was mocking. "No beans?"

"No beans," I said.

"Maybe he has some of that white lightning around."

"I bet he has. Listen, get off your horse, will you? I'm sorry about last night. Do what you have to do, but have you got to ride me all the time?"

"Last night's all right, except for that bra. I can understand last night."

"But you can't believe what I told you."

She hesitated. "No. Not that."

"You'll find out it's the truth. Today."

"How?"

"Because it's going to come out anyway, when you tell. So I can go in there today and shoot him and not be afraid to let people find out about it. Because it's going to come out anyway."

She set the coffee cup down. Over behind the counter the eggs and the ham were sizzling on the grill.

"You're just going to walk in there and shoot him?"

"I told you. I couldn't do it before because they'd find out about Lucy. But now I can because they'll find out anyway. That way is better than nothing."

"Not a hell of a lot. How did you say they do it in this state? Gas chamber?"

"Electric chair."

"A fine distinction," she said. "Real fine."

"I killed Lucy, too. Maybe I deserve it for that. I don't know."

We sat there for a while, not saying anything, drinking the coffee and watching the boy behind the counter. Then he brought the food and we ate. I put away the ham and the eggs and wanted more, only I knew I had had enough. I wanted more but I just couldn't eat.

"You were hungry," she said, when I had finished.

"You did all right, too."

"I love waffles. Listen, I'll make you a bargain."

"About what?"

"About Stewart. I think you're lying. I've seen a lot of worse lies told better. But I'll make you a bargain, if you really mean that about killing him."

"Shoot."

"Hold off one day. Just till tonight."

"So you can get into town and hunt up the Sheriff and try to get me put away?"

"That's my part of the bargain. I'll hold off a day, too."

"What good will it do?"

"I might get to believing you."

"And you might not call the cops at all?"

"I might not."

I thought it over, but I couldn't find her angle. It can't do any harm, I thought.

"Done," I said.

We got up to go then. She had to pay and the boy looked us over again. He couldn't get over the beard and the eye. He gave her the change and she started to turn away and then stopped.

"You got a girl, sonny?"

He blinked. "Yeah ... yes'm. I got a girl."

"You grow a beard," she said. "A black one, down to here. Then you sock her one in the eye and then both of you go look in a mirror. Maybe you'll get enough of it then." Then she tossed him a dime.

He didn't like that. But he didn't know anything to do about it and we went on out to her car.

"I can walk back," I said.

She didn't put up any argument, just got in and started the engine.

"How will I know?"

"I'll be out sometime tonight."

She let in the clutch and the car pulled away and went on down the highway toward town.

You damn fool, I thought. You damn fool. You're going to have cops on your neck in an hour. You don't even know she has any letters, or that she'll keep the bargain, or even why she made it. You damn fool.

I could go on into town now and do it. I wouldn't even need the rifle. I could do it today.

I turned around and started walking back to the shack again. I walked fast and I went right on by the farmhouse where I got my liquor, not even looking at it.

It was dark when she came back. By then, I knew she had kept the bargain. But I didn't know whether she would come back or not, because if she had decided not to believe me, then she wouldn't have to come. She could just wait until tomorrow and go on to them, knowing that I would already be on my way into town.

Then the lights came over the dune, and pretty soon the old car, the two beams converged on me there in the door of the shack. The car came closer, then stopped, and the lights died away. She got out and came across the sand toward me.

She had on a skirt now, falling straight from her hips, and a white blouse, with a collar standing up high against her neck, and she carried a pocketbook beneath her arm and she might have been any girl, anywhere, paying a social call, instead of the girl she was coming to where she was.

"Well, Miss Cummings," I said, and waited for her to notice.

"Let's go in," she said shortly, and she brushed by me and on into the lamplit shack and I followed and again I waited for her to notice. But she sat down in the rough chair and crossed her legs and took a packet of letters out of her bag. She held them in one hand and tapped them into the palm of the other and she didn't have to tell me what they were.

I went over and sat down on the bunk.

"So you decided to come back?"

"Yes."

"That means you believe me."

Her eyes, turning to mine, were almost blank, and her face wore a slight frown. Almost idly, as if she were thinking of something else, she said, "I saw him. I don't think Lucy would have given him a tumble."

I didn't say anything.

She went on tap-tap-tapping the letters in her hand, not looking at me, and I lay back on the bunk and put my hand behind my head. It was her play now and I had all night. I had all the time in the world.

She might at least have noticed, I thought. Not that I did it for her. But she could say something about it.

Maybe then, while I was thinking that, she noticed. "You shaved," she said.

I nodded.

"And washed."

"All over, no less. Don't drink out of the spring for a day or two. I sat in it."

"Your face is too lean and you're too thin. Taller than I would have thought. But I can see why Lucy went for you. I couldn't from the pictures."

"Cut it out. There weren't any pictures."

"I mean the ones she sent me. In these." She looked at the letters. "All right. I believe you."

I sat up and looked at her.

"Because of two things. When I told you Lucy was afraid you'd find out something she didn't want you to know, you were genuinely surprised. And then in that cafe. You meant what you said about killing him. I knew it then. I could feel it. That's why I believe you."

"I still mean it."

"And you're going to do it?"

"Tomorrow."

"And you're going to the chair for it."

"Probably."

"And you say you're not carrying a torch for her."

I swung my legs off the bed.

"Maybe I am," I said. "God, how would I know? I gave her everything. I loved that woman. I would have moved to Alaska if that's where she wanted to go. It was only when she was dead that I knew how she must have hated that farm. But she could have told me. We could have fixed it up; She didn't have to—Not with Stewart. God, how would I know?"

"So it's not the torch."

"It's not the torch. If there is one."

"It's because you're a man and your pride's hurt, isn't it?"

"Yes," I said. "It's that. And it's because he shouldn't have done it, because nobody should do that to anybody. And it's because of something else, too. It's because Lucy's dead on account of him."

"Yes. It's that, too. That's what it is with me."

I didn't get it at first, because it was so deadpan. I thought she was speaking in general terms and I said:

"When did you know her?"

"In New York. Before you married her."

"You must have been close to her, the way you talk."

"I know this: I know there was some reason why she—went to bed with him. I know she loved you more than anything in the world. I don't know what it was. But something made her do it. Something we don't know about."

"It was the farm," I said. "She hated living there. That must have been it. She must have got to hating me too."

She got up and walked to the door and looked out.

"You poor fool," she said. "You never even knew her. You didn't know a thing about her." She turned around and leaned back against the doorjamb and looked at me. I could see the faint purple of her eye under the powder. I was waiting for her to tell me and beginning to pull in my belly against the hurt of it.

Chapter Eleven

"She was just a kid waitress in a little joint where a bunch of us used to eat. Just a painted little blonde with big eyes and no more sense than a rabbit.

"But there was something about her, something the other painted little rabbits didn't have. Maybe it was the way she talked, not harsh and full of Bronx. Maybe the way she smiled all over her face, sort of eager to please, like a puppy dog.

"Anyway, I liked her. I was working in a show then—that was just a line I was giving you about writing—and I was doing O.K. and I always managed a bigger tip than usual for her. I could figure she needed it, working in a place like that.

"So one day I went in at the regular time and the kid wasn't there. I keep calling her a kid. I guess actually she wasn't but maybe a year or two younger than I was." Jean's face grew suddenly harsh. "But I was a lot older than she was in other ways. Even then.

"I didn't think much about it, but when for three days I didn't see her, I went to the manager and asked him what happened to the little blonde, the one they called Lucy."

"He looked at me sort of sour. 'I had to give her the boot,' he said. 'She got herself in trouble.'"

I didn't say anything. I just sat and listened to her. Each one of the words was a blow from a hammer, each one hit me separately, but I kept on pulling in my belly and sucking at the air. I didn't say anything or even move. She was still leaning against the doorjamb, her hands behind her, when she began to speak again.

"I don't know. It happens to thousands of decent kids every year. It wasn't anything to blow my stack over. But I don't know. It got to me somehow, thinking about that eager, what-comes-next little face. Anyway, he gave me her name and address and I went around to the dump where she lived.

"It was a furnished room on about the fourth or fifth floor of an old house in a slum neighborhood. Like the one I grew up in. I felt right at home going up all those stairs. I think I could have gone up them blindfolded.

"I found the right door and knocked on it, but there wasn't any answer. I stood there, all decked out in a new outfit I was wearing for the first time, clean and smart and pretty, and looked around me at that dark hall and smelled the fried meat and the old dust and the unwashed people, and I thought, This is what you got away from, sister. This is what you worked and lied and cheated and sweated to get away from. You better clear out of here now before you get the smell of it all over you again and never get it off.

"But I knocked again. There wasn't any answer this time, either. So I opened the door and walked in. She hadn't even locked it.

"She was crouched in the window, with her back to me. I don't think she even heard the knocking or the door opening or me coming in. She just crouched there on the sill, like a bag of old clothes stuffed into the window to keep the rain out.

"Something told me not to scream or speak or do anything to frighten her. I stepped out of my shoes and tiptoed across the room. I noticed that the bed was made up and everything was very neat. It was funny, almost, the room so neat and clean and her there in the window like that.

"I was right up behind her then and I reached out and put both my arms around her waist and I sort of whispered, Don't be afraid. Just come in here and tell me about it, now.

"I thought she'd try to jump then, when I got my arms around her, and I was all braced to hang on and stop her if she put up a battle. But there wasn't any battle. There wasn't anything. She didn't even move. She just kept on crouching there as stiff as a statue. Well, I started pulling at her and still she didn't fight or anything, and pretty soon I got her out of the window and over on the bed.

"She was in some kind of shock, I guess. She just lay there, hardly even breathing. There was a glass of water by the bed. I wet my handkerchief and kept bathing her face, talking easy and gentle to her. Pretty soon she began to come around.

"Her eyes got real scared, her face screwed all up, and then she began to cry. I've seen the time I needed to cry myself, so I just sat there and let her get it all out of her. It was pretty terrible.

"I sat there and pretty soon the crying started to die down. Then it stopped and she turned her head and looked at me. Her eyes were wide and scared and sort of unbelieving.

"'The fence,' she whispered. 'The fence.'

"I didn't get it at first. But she kept whispering it, over and over, like it was something she had to make me understand. And finally I understood. I got up and went to the window and leaned out and there it was. The fence, four stories below. It was one of those old fences with iron palings, sharp and pointed, and it was right under her window.

"There was a piece of paper fluttering on top of it but not blowing away. Right through the middle of it was one of those palings, sharp and black and waiting, and all the rest of the fence there too, waiting, like a row of teeth sharpened with a file.

"I heard her whisper behind me, 'I was going to jump. And then the fence was there looking at me. I couldn't move all of a sudden. I couldn't even think. I could just see those spikes, waiting for me. And I couldn't move.'

"'Don't talk about it,' I said. 'It's all right now.'

"Well, that was a long time ago, and she's dead now. But maybe you understand why, that day in Belleview, when I read about her committing suicide in the papers, I knew it wasn't so. Why, if there was a bullet hole in her head, I knew somebody else had put it there.

"Because bullets are spikes, too. Aren't they, Harry?"

She still had not moved away from the door. I felt my fingernails biting into my palms.

"Yes," I said. "Bullets are spikes, too."

"You're beginning to see, aren't you? Beginning to see how much there was about her you never even dreamed of."

"Go on," I said. "I want to hear it all."

"There's not much more. I took her in with me and took care of her. Her folks were dead and she'd come to New York to get on the stage. They all come to get on the stage."

"Like you?"

"No. I grew up there. But I guess I wanted the stage as bad as she did. As they all do."

"I thought she was born there, too."

"I know. We gave her a new background. We gave her a second start—not just another effort, but a whole new life. We planned it together during those months we waited for the baby. I figured it was too late for me—I'd seen too much, done too much to start over. But with her—well, the trouble she was in was just one of those things. She got caught the first time. With some zoot-suit Broadway cowboy. Because he told her he could get her a spot in a night club. She never even saw him again to tell him he was a papa. And it was the first time for her."

"All right," I said. "Goddamnit, all right!"

"It makes you squirm, doesn't it? A lot of things are falling into place, aren't they?"

"Go on," I said. "You can't say anything I'm not saying to myself."

"I taught her how to wear clothes, how to walk and make herself up and wear her hair. When the baby came, I arranged to have it taken to the adoption home, the best one in the city. Well, after the baby, you wouldn't have known her. It's like that for some women. She had been skinny, but now she filled out and her skin got that peaches-and-cream look a girl would give her soul for. I had saved up some money and we spent it all outfitting her. And then I got her a job in a department store, modeling, after I talked her out of trying the stage again."

"Why? Why did you do all that for her?"

"Then I got a chance to do a tour with a USO show and I took it. While I was gone I got a letter from her saying she was married to you. When I got back to New York, you were overseas. I could see she was in seventh heaven, and I guess maybe right then I was as happy as I'm ever going to be in this world."

"Why?" I said again. "Why all this for her?"

She closed her eyes. She hadn't moved from the doorjamb since she started her story.

"It was almost as if she were my younger sister, the way we came to feel about each other. She was a clean kid, with a nice clean uncluttered mind. She was kind and she liked to laugh, and she went to church every Sunday. She was the sort of person I'd never known before.

"And she loved that baby. It took me months to convince her it was best to place the child with the adoption people. Even then it was only because she realized what life would have been for little Jean—she named her for me—that she decided to do it. She didn't care for herself. It nearly broke her heart when she finally made up her mind to do it."

I noticed how quiet the night had suddenly grown. Her voice was the only sound you could hear. Even the crickets, I thought, even the crickets are listening to her.

"And then after she was married—well, I guess it proved something," she said. Her voice cracked as if her throat had gone dry with the long recital.

"It proved girls like Lucy and me had a chance after all. It showed you could find what you wanted without stealing and cheating and sleeping with people who could help you, getting old before your time and even then not finding it. Maybe because I felt like I had done all those things already and couldn't go back. But I had kept her out of it. I had proved something, to myself, through her. I guess that was it."

I didn't say anything. I had never known such shame as I did then, at the remembrance of the cowardice and the weakness and the self-pity in which I had wallowed for two years. If I could wipe it all out, I thought, if I could make it like it had never been …

"Because, you see, I wasn't any Ethel Merman. I was just another cutie in the line, maybe a solo dance every now and then, but never anything big. And it didn't look as if there ever would be anything big.

"But right then, while I was back in New York, I got a chance to go to South America with a show, one of the leads. It looked like my big break. I should have known better, I should have known there weren't any big breaks for little Jean. But I went.

"The show folded in São Paulo and I was flat broke. I didn't even get my last week's pay. So I took a job in a little joint there, dancing, and that's where I was when the letters stopped coming from Lucy.

"I had written her that I had a swell job, because I didn't want to spoil anything for her. The two of you were out on the Coast when I first landed there, and then you were back on your farm and then the letters stopped coming.

"At first, I was saving every penny to get home. After she quit writing, I figured she had just sort of forgotten about me and I felt pretty bad about it. I just stayed on down there. But finally I got sick of it and I had enough money and I took a plane. I landed in New York three weeks ago.

"Well, I put in a call to Lucy, for old times' sake. That was when I found out she was dead, and that you couldn't be reached by phone."

There was no more emotion in it than in the Sears, Roebuck catalogue, but I listened to each dull syllable of it. I wanted to run out into the night, to lose myself in darkness, but I forced myself to stay there on the bunk, stay there and listen.

"I bought that old car and drove to Belleview, the nearest town of any size to St. John's I could find on the map, and went to the library and looked it up in the papers. That was when I knew it wasn't suicide and that somebody had killed her.

"I got a hotel room. I didn't leave it for two days, trying to figure it out. And I remember three things. I remembered she told me in New York about your wedding night. How when you—found something missing, you flew into a rage and she had to lie about having had an accident when she was a little girl to keep you from walking out."

"But I believed her," I said. "I believed everything she told me!"

"Sure. You believed her finally. And after I remembered that, I remembered what she had said in one of her letters. That she sometimes thought if you ever found out about the baby you'd kill her. For deceiving you."

"I was always so sure," I said. "There was right and there was wrong. I didn't know anything about anything."

"No," she said, "you didn't. And then there was the last thing. If that home had ever placed the baby somewhere, they'd have notified Lucy. Not where, or to whom, but just that it had been adopted and was well and happy. So suppose they had notified her. Only suppose you opened the letter first and found out about it all."

"So you decided I killed her."

"Yes. And I came over here to see you, what you were like, before I went to the police and tried to get them to believe me. Because I knew how much she loved you. Because if she could love you all that much, how could you have killed her?"

"That's a laugh," I said. "She loved me a lot, all right. Enough to go to bed with Dick Stewart."

"She loved you. I don't know why she did that. There was some reason. I know there was. Maybe he found out some way about the baby, threatened her. I don't know how, but maybe that was it. She would have done it to keep you from finding out about the baby."

"I should have listened to her," I said. "Maybe that was what she was trying to tell me."

"It must have been. Because I know—I tell you I *know*—she loved you more than anything." She tossed the letters in my lap. "These will prove it."

"One other thing," I said. "The trunk. What were you looking for?"

"The letter from the adoption home. If I could find that, then I'd know. It would prove you knew about the baby. It would be something the police might believe. But there wasn't any letter."

I nodded absently. Then I opened the letters and began to read them. And I saw that Jean was right. Oh, there was no poetry or undying protestations or romantic nonsense. They were just letters, the kind any girl might write to an older sister. But it was there, between every line, after every period, in every word. Lucy had loved me, had wanted only for me to be happy. When I finished those letters, there wasn't any doubt of that.

And I had killed her.

Maybe two or three years before I would have said something or done something. Maybe I would have squared it away inside of me and got it straight and picked up what there was left of it and gone on to somewhere, somehow.

But not now. Because there was but one thing I had to turn to now, and I reached down under the bed and got out the fruit jar and took a drink.

"That's got to stop," she said.

"Go to hell."

"If I'm going to help you do it, that's got to stop."

I set the jar down carefully.

"Come again," I said.

"If I'm going to help you kill Stewart, you've got to cut out the whisky."

"If you're ..." I got up and walked over to her. She didn't move, but her face told it to me again. "How?"

"Not like you said. Not just walk in and shoot him."

"You're wrong. There isn't any other way."

"That's why the whisky has to go."

"You go on," I said. "You beat it the hell back to where you came from."

"No. We're going to do it. And we're going to get away with it."

"But why? Why you?"

She moved away from me then and stood in the middle of the floor and looked off into far places I had never seen.

"Because he wrecked it. I don't know how or why, but he tore it all down, the dream house. He wrecked everything I had worked and schemed to get for her. He caused her to die. He ruined everything. And when he did it, he ruined everything for me, too."

"Yes," I said. "For me, too. He's ruined everything."

"And now we're going to kill him."

I picked up the fruit jar and walked over to the door and threw it as far as I could.

"Maybe there is a way," I said. "Maybe we can find it."

Chapter Twelve

I stood there in the door and I could feel her get up and come across the floor to me. She was right behind me.

"I don't want to die," she said.

"I don't either. Not now."

"Did you before?"

"I didn't care."

"It's got to be right, then. There can't be any mistakes."

"There won't be."

"You've got to keep off the whisky. You've got to eat right and sleep right and get to be a man again. You've got to get your nerves back. You were shaking like a leaf yesterday. You've got to be a man again."

"I will be."

"How soon?"

I turned around then and put my hand on her neck.

"I could start right now."

Her eyes narrowed.

"I need you," I said. "I need to know I can be a man with a woman again."

Her eyes seemed to glaze over.

"I hate you, Harry. I hate you for being so bullheaded, and so sure you were right, and for not listening to her that night. I hate you for not even trying to know anything about her except that she was yours, your property. I hate you because you didn't even try to find out if maybe what you saw, what she did, wasn't for some reason. You didn't even give her a chance."

"And you hate me because of the way you saw me yesterday."

"Yes. That too. And then you ask me what you did."

"Because I need you. And I'm going to have you."

"Yes. You need me."

She moved away, toward the bunk, and then she kicked her loafers off and her hands went toward her side and the skirt fell around her feet. She began to unbutton the blouse and then that, too, was at her feet and the slip was coming over her head.

She threw that on the chair and then I fumbled at the hook on her brassiere. She stood there and let me take it off. Then she stepped out of her pants and I picked her up and put her down on the bunk.

Her breasts were hard and almost flat and her legs cold and her stomach unresisting. Her lips were flaccid under mine and she was like a dead woman. But the fire was in me now, two years of loneliness and wanting boiled in me, and I couldn't stop.

At first she didn't even close her eyes. And then, later, I heard her whisper, "You son of a bitch."

Her eyes closed then and I felt the movement of her, her hands on my back, feverish, clutching. Finally the hate or fear or revulsion set her free, set all of her free. We were fused, welded together by some inhuman hand, some hand coming from out of the darkness to encircle us. I heard her whispering the same thing over and over in my ear. Then there was not even the whispering any more, just the wanting and the having. Then the one final, unbelievable, immemorial having, and then the night with the crickets heard again, and the air stirring across us, and the lonely rending bay of a hound, somewhere beyond the dunes.

I woke up the next morning knowing it. For the first time in months I woke up and there wasn't any whisky taste in my mouth, my head was free and clear, and the air smelled clean in my nostrils. I woke up and lay there enjoying it, and I knew the plan.

I hadn't thought about it or dreamed it or anything, it was just there, a presence, a realization, and I knew this was it, the only way, and that the long search was over. I stretched comfortably and chuckled.

Then I realized she wasn't beside me. I sat up in sudden panic. She had to be there, everything hinged on her now. I leaned forward to look out the door and with relief saw the old car, forlorn in the sand, already gleaming under the morning sun.

I got up and put on my clothes and went outside. She was down by the spring, in slacks again, just sitting there in the shade with a hand trailing in the water.

"Good morning," I called. Her head turned my way but she didn't say anything and I walked over to her.

"You're up early," she said.

"I don't usually get to sleep so soon at night."

There was a moment of embarrassment then, and I took the gourd off the nail driven in one of the trees and dipped up water and drank it. When I looked back at her it was all right again.

"You want to go get some breakfast again?"

"I brought some things. Coffee, bread. They're in the car."

I eased down in the sand beside her.

"Then you knew you were going to stay?"

"I thought I might have to."

"You mean you thought I might make you stay?"

The brown eyes flashed at me. "Well, didn't you?"

"I don't think so. You could have left any time. Before or after."

She laughed, bitterness creeping into the flat sound of it.

"What I told you about myself. That didn't have a thing to do with it, I guess."

"I didn't even think of anything like that."

"I'll bet. You know, it's a funny thing. Every time I need some help from a man, they want to charge the same price you did."

"I'm sorry. But I told you. I needed you. Maybe for my pride, to make me feel like a man again. Or maybe just because I wanted you so much. What you might have done before didn't enter into it."

She laughed. "But you knew I'd have to do it," she said. "You knew I needed your help, too. And you knew I was used to paying for what I need."

"No," I said. "You're all mixed up. I ..."

She stood up, in one quick supple movement, and brushed her wet hand against the slacks.

"Come on. Let's get some coffee."

We scoured out my crusted old coffeepot and I fired up the Cadet heater and before long the coffee smell was making my mouth water. She made toast in the skillet and produced a jar of grape jelly from the car and by that time the coffee was done. I never had a better breakfast.

I pushed back my second cup of coffee and sighed.

"I didn't know how I missed that stuff."

She poured herself another cup of coffee.

"Well," she said, "do you think you're ready to start pulling yourself together? Because you've got to, you know, or it will never work."

"Then you still mean it? You're still going through with it?"

"Things look different in the daytime," she said. "I got up this morning and went out there and sat down and started thinking. My God, I thought, here I am planning to kill a man, just because of what he did to another woman. Be logical, I told myself. If you want to kill this Stewart, then you have to kill London too. They were both in it, both of them helped cause it."

She sipped at the coffee.

"But then I thought, London's a souse and he's had his arm shot off to boot. In a way he's paid up.

But this Stewart. He got off scot free. He hasn't paid a nickel."

"So we'll make him pay."

"Yes."

The viciousness in her voice startled me. For a moment the brown eyes were unholy with hate. The words were flat and calm, the more ominous for being so. I'm glad it's him, I thought, I'm glad it's not me. I spoke slowly:

"Then I'll tell you how we're going to do it…

She sat there a long time without moving. She had heard me out, silently, no signs of pleasure, agreement, shock on the tanned face. The air in the shack was still and warm and outside the only sound was the monotonous repetition of a mockingbird. I never heard him sing in the daytime before, I thought. It must be a sign.

She got up and stepped to the door and hooked her thumbs in the slacks.

"It would work, all right," she said.

"Like a charm. He'd go for it hook, line, and sinker."

"He would. Only you've got to think of something else, because I won't do it."

"What? I don't understand."

"I won't do it, I said."

I came up behind her.

"You come in here giving me all that tough stuff," I said. "You tell me how you're going to help me. Then I come up with a foolproof idea and you chicken out on me."

"There are other ways."

"Not this good."

"There must be."

"For God's sake," I said. "Do you hate me that much?"

She turned and looked at me evenly and Judgment Day was in her face.

"Maybe I do."

"All right. So up till yesterday I was living on corn whisky and beans and not washing. But that's not what it is. You want me to think, but that's not it, not by a damn sight."

Her hand flashed at my face and I caught her wrist and held it.

"I'll tell you what it is. It's because I got in bed with you and you enjoyed it. That's it, isn't it?"

She struggled against my grip and I laughed.

"That's the real ticket, isn't it? You learned to hate men a long time ago, from the ones you had to give it to, to get what you wanted. And you hate them all. Especially the ones you give it to."

I laughed again and she stopped fighting. She backed up against the wall and her eyes became wide and shifty.

"So when you had to give it to somebody to get yourself out of a jam, or to get something out of him, or maybe just because you got to the point sometimes where you wanted it yourself, you had to have it yourself, you really hated that somebody, didn't you? And when you enjoy it, like last night, it's worse. Because you don't understand that. So you hate those times and those men—like me— worst of all. Or maybe I'm the only one it's ever been like that with."

She stood quietly then and the shiftiness went out of her eyes. Her bosom was heaving a little higher now and I started to laugh. Then I stopped and turned away and sat down on the bunk.

"You don't need to worry. That's not in the plan. You want my word on it, you can have it."

For a long time, I thought she hadn't heard me. And then her voice, smaller now, inched hesitantly across the still room.

"What happens afterward? After we kill him?"

"For God's sake, what do you think? You go your way, I go mine. We'll split the dough."

"I don't want any of the money."

"Why not?"

"I'm not in it for money. Just to kill him is all I want."

"That's mighty Christian of you. Mighty Christian."

A flash of the old fire was back in her voice.

"You can have the damn money. I won't ever want any of it."

"But you're in?"

"Yes. I'm in." Again the flatness, the calm, the brooding, implacable words.

"And do you want my word on the other?" I said.

"It wouldn't be any good. You mean what you say now. You probably won't tomorrow. I'll take my chances."

I got up and went back over to her.

"My word's good," I said. "That didn't go with the whisky. That's one thing I have left. I'll keep my hands—hand—off."

She smiled then, I could not tell whether in mockery or amusement.

"Men," she said. "You beat them, kick them, do anything to them. But they still hang on to something they call pride. Being filthy didn't hurt your pride, or being a coward. But when I just hint your word's no good, you get up on your hind legs. That's what you call pride."

"And what do you call it?"

"I don't know. Not pride, though. Conceit, maybe."

I laughed.

"The hell with pride," I said. "I'll go out to the spring while you change. On an occasion like this, you want to look your best. Pride or no pride."

Chapter Thirteen

We came out on the broad porch and stood there a minute and looked at the green lawn and the cars going past on the street, and for the first time since I had hurled that fruit jar into the darkness the night before, I wanted a drink. I wanted one bad.

"Well, that's over," I said.

"It was so quick. I didn't know it could be done that fast anywhere."

"They make a business of it in this state. It has to be quick to satisfy the kind of trade they get."

She laughed, and the sound was almost mirthful. But not quite. I took her arm and we went down the steps. I still wanted that drink.

I looked down at her as we walked along. She hardly came to my chest, even in the high heels she had put on for the occasion, and the little hat she had dug up from somewhere perched on top of her blonde head. The faint purple bruise was hardly visible under her make-up. She wore a summer-weight suit of some light yellow material and I decided it was just right for her. For some reason, I forgot about the drink then and my spirits jumped up a couple of notches.

"Anyway," I said, "you looked the part. I'm sorry about this suit."

My gabardine, a relic of more cheerful days that I had turned up after much rummaging in the trunk, hung on me in ungraceful folds. I hadn't realized I'd lost so much weight. Before, it had fitted my frame as if it had been made specially for me, which it had. I had had to tuck the left sleeve in the coatpocket, and two years in the trunk had put it in definite need of a press job, which it had not yet had. But it was clean, anyway.

"Never mind the suit," she said. "It's more than I would have expected of you."

"I'm not going to quarrel with you," I said. "You don't like me. O.K. But we have a job to do, and until we get it done you just shoot off that pretty mouth of yours all you want to. You don't bother me a bit."

"Go to hell," she said.

We walked into the downtown district of St. Johns. There was one main street, and the only reason it was paved was because it was also a state highway. You could count maybe a dozen stores of all descriptions, if you looked closely, and a doctor's office, and a couple of lawyers' dens, the mellow old courthouse, a ramshackle newspaper office, and two benches on a corner. Dick Stewart's was the largest of the stores, but it was at the other end of the street from us.

I stopped in front of the street's only dry-goods store.

"Let's go in here a minute," I said.

"What for?"

"I owe you something. Remember?"

"You owe me plenty."

"I mean the bra. The one I tore off you."

"Oh. That. Skip it for now. I'm in no mood to go shopping."

I took her arm again. "Come on," I said. "I possess the grand total of fifteen dollars and seventy-eight cents. That's what's left of the London fortune. It won't take that much, will it?"

"Not in this store. Nothing would. What are you so cheerful about, anyway?"

We were in the store now and I half pulled her with me back to the ladies'-wear section.

"I just woke from the dead," I said. "Why shouldn't I be cheerful about it? What size do you wear?"

"Never mind that. If your heart's set on it, I'll do the buying."

I stood by grinning while she and the salesgirl huddled. When the salesgirl looked at me over her shoulder, I winked at her. She liked that but she hastily started wrapping the package when Jean gave her a dirty look.

"That didn't hurt, did it?" I said, when we came out into the bright sunlight again. "And I still have nearly thirteen bucks."

"Let's get home, buster. I'm dying of the heat in this fancy getup."

"Home," I said. "Who would ever have thought you'd call it that? One more stop, sugar, and we're on our way."

I led her across the street and into the newspaper office. Harvey Jenkins, who had been editing the little weekly as long as I could remember, sat at a littered desk, its pigeonholes dribbling odd papers and pencils, old paste pots and proof sheets.

"Hello, Harvey," I said. "We've got an item for you."

He looked up at us and pushed an ancient green eyeshade back on his forehead. He peered closely at me and I saw at once that he didn't recognize me. Even two years ago, his memory had begun to fail him.

"It's Harry London," I said.

He looked at me a while longer, then swiveled his gaze to Jean's bored face. He leaned forward and spat a bolt of Brown's Mule at the stained baseboard.

"It ain't," he said.

"Yes, it is," I said. "You just haven't seen me in a long time."

"I seen you a month ago, walking right down that street. Leastways, a feller told me it was you. Didn't believe him then, and don't believe you now. Neither one of you looked like Harry London to me."

"It's him, all right," Jean said. "He washed, that's all."

He looked at her sharply. "Who might you be?"

"Who might you be?"

He cackled at that and I smiled too. "You want to see my driver's license, Harvey?"

"Nope. Reckon it's you, all right. Always had a smart lip on you. You decide to come out'n hibernation?"

"Sure did. I have a society note for you."

He pulled a scrawled-on sheet of paper closer and took up a thoroughly chewed stub of pencil. A faint blob of tobacco juice formed in a corner of his mouth. He adjusted the green eyeshade on his brow and looked up at me through it.

"The wedding of Harry London of this county ..." I said, and he started to write and then stopped and looked up at me again, his decrepit jaw sagging. "... and Miss Jean Cummings of New York City ..."

"I be ding-dabbed," he said.

"Go on, write it down." I waited for him to catch up and then I went on: "... was solemnized—isn't that the word they use, Harvey?—at the home of Justice of the Peace Orville Snuggins on the afternoon of July twenty-fifth. The couple will be at home at the former Caldwell farm near St. Johns."

"Don't you dare put that in there," Jean said. "That about being at home at that place."

"That where you goin' to live, Harry?"

"For now," I said.

"Then in it goes," Harvey said. Jean looked angrily at me and I grinned cheerfully.

"I wish I had a picture of the bride," I said, "but that'll have to do."

"A Yankee girl. Ain't you learned your lesson yet, Harry?"

"This one's different."

"They're all alike. That's why I never had one. Won't let a man spit on the walls."

"Why, you old goat," Jean said. "Somebody ought to housebreak you."

He cackled again and tears came in his eyes. "She's got a right smart lip, too," he wheezed.

I laughed and took her arm. We were almost out when he stopped wheezing and cackling and called, "Wait up a minute. You ain't told me nothin' about how—"

"We told you enough," I called back. "After all, this is our wedding day."

I could hear him cackling again as we went on down the street.

"So this is what girls are supposed to hold their breath for," Jean said, as we climbed into her old car. "This is what a wedding day's like."

"Not for all girls," I said. "Just the ones that go around planning to kill people."

I was sitting out by the spring and she was fixing supper. I thought about the way their faces would look when they heard about it, and I almost laughed out loud.

I listened to the noises she was making with pots and pans, and I smelled food smells. You forget how things like that can be, I thought, you forget the good things so easily when the bad ones squeeze in on you.

Imagine me with another wife. After these last years. Imagine me with a woman cooking in the house and the smell of her still in my nostrils and the touch of her on my hand.

And me without a beard. Clean. Sober. And without the face, too. Yes, by God, I haven't seen the face since I told her about it. Imagine that. I never thought I'd see the day again.

I closed my eyes. I forgot, for a moment, the bedrock ugliness on which we had founded this partnership. I forgot, too, the old evil that had foamed in brain and memory these past two years. I forgot all that and maybe somehow I was for that moment the old Harry London again, the one that had lived and loved and laughed so long ago, and I was at peace with myself and her and all the world.

Even with Stewart.

My eyes snapped open. For that moment I hadn't hated him.

It had all been washed away, swept off in peace and the realization, at last, that hate and evil were only a part of the whole, not all of it, that life could go on, that there didn't have to be what had for so long seemed so absolutely, completely, and finally necessary.

But then it was gone, the moment had passed, and with it the old Harry London. You're nuts, I thought. The bastard ought to die. He fouls the very air he breathes.

She came out of the door of the little shack and stood there a moment, looking at me, and then sat down on the rickety stairs.

The sun dropped behind the dunes and the cool night was fast coming down. A bullbat made raucous sounds in a tree on the other side of the spring and the shadows were gone now, and the earth settled into mellow brownness, still and quiet and calm.

I got up and went slowly across the sand toward the shack. There was a smudge of flour on her cheek.

"You look domestic," I said. "Just like a wife."

Her eyes flared at me.

"If that's a funny crack," she said, "you can go to hell."

"All right, all right. Don't be so touchy. I meant it."

Her face softened.

"I'm sorry. It's just that it was all so cold and quick and mechanical." She laughed, a little bitterly. "You know how women are. Maybe I've just heard too much about orange blossoms and organ music."

"I know," I said. I sat down by her on the step.

We sat there a while and watched the night creep in, not saying anything. This is going to be a hell of a thing, I thought, until we get it over with.

Two complete strangers. And the way she feels about me. Better to get it done quickly.

"When are you going into your act?" I said.

She shrugged.

"Soon, I guess. I might as well get started."

"The sooner, the better. He'll know something is up, but he won't know what."

"Maybe I can't get anywhere with him."

"You can't. Not when he finds out you're my wife. He'll smell a rat. But everybody else will believe it. And that's what counts."

"Yes. That's what counts."

When we went inside to eat, I found she had done wonders over the heater, and I told her so. There were hamburgers and boiled potatoes, canned string beans and coffee and a store-bought cake for a dessert. We'd stopped on the way back from St. John's to pick up supplies.

Even so, supper was a glum affair. She hardly touched her food, and long before I was through she had moved again to the doorstep and sat there, gazing out at the velvet night, the faint sheen of the stars, and the rolling sand.

I wheeled around in the chair and looked at her lonely back, the small shoulders hunched slightly, and I wanted to go over and put my arm around her. And then I remembered the pledge I had given her that morning.

"I'm going to fix this place up, Jean," I said. "It'll be at least two weeks we have to live out here. Maybe longer. We might as well be comfortable, I guess."

She didn't say anything and I got up and began to do the dishes. I ought to boot her the hell out of here, I thought. I didn't have any business getting into this.

I ought to have had better sense.

We went to bed early. I didn't remind her of my promise, but I made up a pallet on the floor with two of the three blankets we had and rolled into it without a word of protest from her.

I could hear her breathing across the room. The moon would not be up for a while yet, but my eyes were used to darkness and I could turn my head and see the vague shape of her on the bunk. Sleep was going to be a long time coming, I thought.

"You loved her very much, didn't you, Harry?" Her voice was quiet and even in the vast night.

"Yes," I said.

"Do you still love her?"

"I don't know. I thought I hated her after that night. But now I don't know."

"Not her. You just hated what she did."

"Maybe so," I said. "Go to sleep."

"It was that way because you never really loved her. Just what she was and how she looked and the way she made you feel. If you had really loved her you'd have given her a chance."

"Stop it," I said. "She's dead now. It's all dead. It doesn't do any good to talk about it."

"I think I hate you, Harry."

"Go to sleep," I said.

She didn't say anything for a long time and I lay there waiting for sleep to come. And then I heard her move on the bunk and bare feet padded on the plank flooring.

I turned my head and she was coming across the floor. She stood over me then and I watched her take off her pajamas and let them fall to the floor. And then she was on the pallet beside me and her arms were around me and I felt something hot and moist on my neck.

"Harry!" she whispered.

"I don't want you," I said. "Get away from me."

I felt her soft breasts against my ribs.

"You let me come to you like this. You didn't try to stop me."

"Yes. I—"

"There isn't anything else for us, Harry."

And then all the resistance went out of me and my arm was around her and my lips found her breast and the warm blood in her veins throbbed against me.

It had never been that way before, not with anybody. Her hot, frantic, tortured body exploded against mine. We clung together, beyond space, beyond time, beyond anything but the things our bodies did to each other, without direction or design, powered only by instinct and urge and desperation.

Later, the moon spilled across us there on the floor, and I looked down at her as she slept, her face in darkness, stippled shadows falling across the small round breasts.

This is beyond me, I thought.

She hates me, she hates all men. But she comes to me in the night, shameless, selfless, in complete and abject surrender, in some nameless despair and agony, she comes to me like that, and then when it's over, no word of love or tenderness or even liking yet passed between us, she whispers once before she sleeps:

"No. It didn't happen ... it didn't happen."

Something curled in me at one thought that would not down: that she had given herself to me to make sure that I would remain a part of our scheme—that she had deliberately paid what she thought was my price.

But she had been right about one thing. I knew it then because of what she had given me that night. I had never really loved Lucy. What I had thought was love was only conceit because she had been my property, because I had made her my property.

Because now I know what love is, I thought. Now I know. It's what I feel for this woman who lies naked and sleeping beside me. It's something I never even knew existed in this world or any other. It's what you feel when you are able to do anything and suffer anything and endure anything and give anything, any time, anywhere, for someone else. Or at least it is for me. That's what love is for me.

And suddenly, I knew with a sort of geometric clarity that I would never again want to kill Dick Stewart.

Because for so long that had been all there was to live for: killing him someday, because he had taken something from me for which I had thought only his life could pay.

But now there was something else. Now there was this woman beside me. Now there was something that could not only pay for what I had lost, but that could wipe that loss from the books of my mind and heart and soul as completely as if there had never been a loss at all.

I didn't want to kill Dick Stewart any more. But I would do it.

I would do it because it was what she wanted. Even though she hated me, she had come to me and given all of herself to further and insure and seal forever her determination to scourge him. I would do anything and suffer anything and endure anything and give anything she wanted.

I would do it because I loved her.

And she loved only some ideal that had died with Lucy, some dream, far more vast and sweeping and fierce than my own puny feelings for my wife had been, loved only that and hated me, even while binding me to her with a chain stronger than fine steel. Hated me even then.

Or did she? I didn't know.

It was beyond me.

Chapter Fourteen

This is the way she told it to me:

Three men were seated on the bench under the wooden porch roof in front of the Coshocken General Mercantile Company. Their eyes were quiet and unquestioning and only jaw muscles moved in their faces. They were oddly alike in their worn overalls and sweat-stained hats. One of them spat a stream of tobacco as she approached.

They watched her pass and enter the store and there was still no curiosity in their eyes. For even then, only two days after it happened, they knew. They knew that Harry London had married another Yankee girl, one who had appeared out of nowhere and gone to live with him on the Caldwell place, and they knew now, eying her calmly and completely, but without insult, who she was.

She felt them watching her, and she went past them, her heels clicking on the sidewalk, over which the frame porch roof stood.

She knew, for I had told her, that what they saw would spread until the whole county, without having seen her, would be able to recognize Mrs. Harry London. She moved Ker hips smoothly, and her heels clicked. Her head was up, her breasts firm and high beneath the neckline of her dress, as she went into the store.

He was waiting on a child behind the candy counter. He did not look up as she came in. Far down the dim aisles, a man in shirt sleeves worked at a desk. Plows, feed bags, mule harness, wheelbarrows, and other stock littered the unswept floor, and shelves ran up the walls full of tools, hardware, and bewildering boxes and packets. She stood quietly by the grilled mail window. Stewart was also the town postmaster and his store served the community as post office.

The little boy was examining the candy stock with slow and infinite care. His gaze moved from

striped peppermint to brown horehound to soft
chocolate and on to colored balls of chewing gum
and his lips moved and his eyes were grave in
doubt.

"How much are those?" An incredibly grimy
finger pointed to the balls of gum.

"Two for a penny," Stewart said.

"I'll take six."

Stewart counted six of the balls into a small
bag. As he raised his head, he met her eyes and she
smiled. He stopped in mid-motion and the sack
nearly slipped from his grasp. He licked his lips
and turned back to the child.

"And two cents' worth of them." Again the
finger poked at the glass counter and Stewart took
two peppermint sticks and dropped them in the
bag.

"That be all, Billy?"

"Guess so," Billy said. "That's all this time."

Stewart glanced at her again. His face was calm
now and there was no shiftiness in the eyes. He
took the coins the boy held out and handed him the
bag. The boy took it and went out. Stewart leaned
on the candy counter and looked at her.

"What can I do for you, ma'am?"

"I want to buy a pressure cooker, please."

She moved closer and smiled at him and his
eyes melted a little and they ran over her, pausing
here and there, and he did not move.

"You lie," he said.

She pouted at him. "That's not very nice."

He laughed. Out of the corner of her eye she saw
the man at the desk in the back of the store swing
around.

"What did he send you for … Mrs. London?"

She looked puzzled. "Who?"

"Harry. Your husband."

"I told you. I want to buy a pressure cooker."

She was very close to the counter now and his
eyes dropped to the low neckline and she leaned

forward. The man in shirt sleeves was still watching and she put her face close to Stewart's.

"And I was wondering what a girl does around here for excitement."

She moved away a little then and laughed out loud. Stewart came around the counter and she turned and moved back to the mail window, her hips swaying. He came up behind her.

"He sent you," he said, his voice low and malevolent. "This is one of his tricks."

"What tricks?"

He took her arm and pulled her around to face him and she leaned close to him. He took a quick step back and she saw sweat pop on his brow.

"Listen," he said. "What's he told you about me?"

"Nothing," she said. "I can see for myself."

His face showed his disbelief.

"He's been giving you lies about me," he said.

"Look, mister, I don't even know your name."

"I'm Dick Stewart. You're sure he hasn't said anything about me?"

"Harry doesn't say much about anything."

He looked at her for a long time. Then he relaxed.

"The pressure cookers are over here," he said.

She followed him to a table near the center of the store.

"You sure act funny," she said. "Like you were afraid of me."

"I'm not afraid. I just thought ... These are eight-ninety-five."

She looked at the cookers with little interest.

"You still haven't told me ... Dick."

"Told you what?"

"What a girl does around here. For excitement."

Her voice had risen a little and Stewart glanced hastily at the man at the desk. This time he did not turn around. He sat very straight in his chair, not moving at all.

"I wouldn't know," he said. "You want the cooker?"

"I wanted a little one."

"This is the smallest size there is."

"Well, I don't know much about cooking."

His eyes feasted on her breasts.

"I bet you don't," he said.

The door of the store slammed. They looked up to see a thin woman entering. Jean hastily moved away, as if she had been caught at something. She touched a hand to her hair.

"I'll take this," she said. She pointed at a fifty-pound bag of fertilizer. He looked at her in exasperation.

"Charge it to me," she said.

The woman was near now and Jean stared at her insolently. The woman's glance was hostile.

"Be with you in a minute, Mrs. Hartley," Stewart said.

He wrote a ticket for the fertilizer and stuck the pad in his pocket.

"I'll carry it out for you."

"That'll be sweet, Dick."

He made a noise beneath his breath and hastily bent and heaved the bag to his shoulder.

He started toward the door and she smiled frostily at Mrs. Hartley and followed. Her hips swayed more than necessary under the tight skirt.

"Listen," Stewart murmured when they had passed beyond the thin woman. "You keep away from here. I don't want any truck with that husband of yours."

"I like it here," she said. "I like you."

He swore and pushed open the door.

The old Chevrolet was parked just down the street from the store. He jerked open the door and tumbled the fertilizer to the floor.

The three men still sat beneath the porch roof, apparently not watching, occasionally spitting tobacco juice.

He straightened up and she swayed close to him. One hip brushed against his leg.

"Thank you," she whispered, "for everything."

"You go to hell," he murmured.

She moved even closer and her breasts now almost touched him. As if drawn by a magnet, his eyes dropped to her neckline. Then, with another low curse, he jerked around and went back to the store.

"See you tomorrow," she called after him, quite clearly, and laughed.

One of the men spat again and stood up and silently moved away.

"I feel dirty," she said, when she had finished telling it. "That man. Ugh!"

"You did fine," I said. "That ought to get the ball rolling good. Old Joe Buxton, the bookkeeper, and Lena Hartley, and whoever the three men were. That ought to start things off with a bang."

"I felt like a prostitute," she said. "All that paint and throwing myself at him like that."

"It won't be for long."

"He was scared. He tried to act mean, but I could see how scared he was."

"He's got reason," I said. "He knows it's no coincidence. Not twice, he knows it wouldn't happen twice, not after that night, anyway. But he won't figure it until it's too late, until we lower the boom on him."

"You know," she said, "when he looked down my dress like that, I wanted it to be right then. He's from under a rock."

"If you didn't know what you do, he wouldn't be so bad, would he?"

"I don't know. He's handsome, all right. And those bedroom eyes and those hands. But I don't think I'd like him even then. That's what I can't understand about Lucy. That's why I know there must have been something we don't know about."

We didn't say anything for a while, sitting there in the night, on the sand in front of the shack. It was pretty nice, I thought; you have to hand it to women. They make a place a lot nicer. Just to have one around, to know she's nearby, and to see the skirt swirl at her knees, and the smooth skin, and the faint woman smell.

"What are you thinking about, Jean?"

"Oh ... I was remembering something Lucy wrote in one of those letters, after she married you."

"What was that?"

"She said something about she had been out hunting with you. It wasn't anything much. But I was thinking how she said she had been hunting with you and then all the rest of that part of the letter was about you, how many birds you killed, what a good shot you were. Not a word about herself."

"I remember," I said.

"That was like her. To show that she was happy, not because of what she herself was doing, but because of what you were doing. To be happy because you were happy."

"Yes," I said. "That was like her."

"I wonder if she's happy now."

"You keep talking as if she were alive," I said.

"I know. But I got to thinking ..."

"About last night?"

"Yes."

Something savage bit at me.

"What do you want me to do?" I said. "Get down and pray a little and ask her to forgive us?"

I felt her whole body tighten up beside me. I wished I could call the words back.

"I'm sorry," I said. "That was a lousy thing to say."

I didn't tell her that I barked out the harsh words because she had touched a sore spot. In the daylight, the night before seemed unreal, and all

that day I had remembered my feelings then with
a sense of betrayal.

You get a woman in your bed again, I had
thought, and right away you forget Lucy, forget the
woman you loved and killed, forget the two years
you went through a living suicide, forget
everything, even the debt you have to pay, and tell
yourself it's because you're in love with a cheap
bitch you've slept with twice in the three nights
you've known her. A fine avenger you are.

But I hadn't quite convinced myself. I couldn't
dismiss it that easily. And her words had pointed
up the puzzle in my brain.

"Listen," she said. "I told you how it was. What
you and Lucy had between you meant something to
me. More than you could know. It meant that such
things—oh, I know it's corny, but such things as
love and home and happiness really existed. And
now she's dead and I ..."

"All right," I said. "It doesn't have to happen
again. Maybe it's best that way. Maybe we ought to
just keep our minds on the job."

She turned her head slowly to look at me. Then
she laughed, bitterly.

"We have got a job to do, haven't we?" she said.

Have we? I thought. Goddamnit. Have we? I
don't know. I don't know anything any more.

I could hear her breathing, slowly and evenly,
and when I turned my head, I could see the vague
shape of her on the bunk. When she moved, I heard
the dry mattress crackle.

I couldn't sleep. I lay there on the floor and tried
to straighten it all out in my mind. About Lucy.
About Stewart. About the strange, hard, lost
woman sleeping a few feet away from me.

But it all whirled in my mind like a carrousel,
going round and round and round and never
getting anywhere. Because under it all, around it
all, over it all, the desire and the longing in me for
Jean swirled and screamed.

I got up and stepped across the floor and stood there looking down at her. And then I saw that her eyes were open and that she was looking at me too.

"I could hear you breathing," I said. My voice cracked on the last word.

"I could hear you too." The pale white oval of her face seemed to swim toward me.

"Every time you moved," I said, "I'd have to remember you were there."

"And every time I turned my head I could see you lying there on the floor." There was an incredulous sort of wonder in her voice.

"It's no use," I said. "Is it?"

"No, it's no use."

"Like you said last night, there isn't anything else for us."

I bent down and pulled back the thin blanket.

And then I heard the dry mattress crackle under me, too, and felt her warm hands touch me.

Chapter Fifteen

It was over a week later, and Jean was again spending the afternoon in town. I was sitting at the shelf at the back wall of the cabin, working on the letter. I wanted to be careful with it, to watch out for slips, and this was the sixth one I had composed.

For our plan, it was a good thing Brax Jordan had put Lucy's typewriter in the trunk two years ago. He had said it was too old to sell and that I could throw it away if I didn't want it. I had been furious, but soon I had forgotten it. And now it was coming in handy.

Then I heard the sound of the car, not the rattle of the old Chevvy, but a smooth hum, a powerful engine pulling through the sand. I got up quickly, put the typewriter in the trunk, and went to the door.

I leaned against the jamb and watched the car pull up.

It was a Buick, a new one. Brax Jordan looked like a gnome inside the huge mass of metal. Then he got out and came across the sand.

"Come in the house," I said.

He stopped a yard or two away. "Where is she?"

"You mean Jean?"

"I mean whatever-her-name-is that didn't have any more sense than to marry you. If what I hear is right."

I laughed. "Good ol' Brax. Never spares his clients' feelings. You coming in or just standing there?"

"It'll be too hot inside. Let's get over in the shade."

We went over and sat down by the spring and I handed him the gourd and he took a long drink of the cool water and handed the gourd back. Then he lit up a long cigar.

"You off the hooch, Harry?"

"Yes. And I shave and wash and eat right and sleep right and brush my teeth."

"Then there's that much to her credit. Who is she?"

"A writer. She read something about me in an old newspaper an came out to see me."

"And it was love at first sight?"

"Something like that."

He laughed.

"I bet it was," he said. "Where is she now?"

"In town."

A faint shadow crossed his face. I wonder if he's already heard them talking, I thought.

"They tell me she's a knockout."

"Not like Lucy. Not that much of a knockout."

He leaned forward.

"Listen, Harry. I've got it figured this way. It was like with a child eating candy. The child loves the stuff, he doesn't know why, it pleases him some way, but he can't stop, he isn't able to ask himself if it's good for him, if he ought to eat so much of it. So he goes on eating it if his ma isn't there to paddle his bottom. And then he gets too much of it and throws it up all over himself."

"I don't get it," I said.

"It was that way with you. The way you were living. You finally threw it up all over yourself, and right then, there she was, and you married her because that seemed like a way to begin to get out of it."

"Yes," I said. "Maybe. I don't know."

He blew the cigar smoke in my face and leaned back again against the tree. His small feet were placed precisely together.

"That much figures," he said. "Everybody is thinking that. But listen, Harry. Think about this. Why did she marry you?"

"You think about it. You want to know."

"You are asking me to believe," he said, "that this girl, this Yankee girl at that, who is completely alien to this country, these people, all this"—his hand waved vaguely around him—"who looks like something out of a Grade B movie, who obviously has known men and money and excitement—you are asking me to believe that such a creature drove in here and out of whatever compulsions women feel took up with and married a man who at that time was not only a drunk and a pauper, but who was also dirty, underfed, hardly human, and damn near crazy, and who could not even offer her a roof that didn't leak or a mattress on which to lay her head."

"That roof doesn't leak," I said, "and I'm not asking you to believe anything. You want to see the certificate?"

"Never mind. I've talked to Snuggins."

"Then let it be," I said. "In the first place, you can see it's good for me. In the second place, stranger things have happened. In the third place, it's none of your business in the fourth place."

He puffed at the cigar. His eyes narrowed.

"All right, Harry. I'm your lawyer. God help me. I will concede it could have happened. I will even concede that you believe it happened just the way it looks. But not her. No. I don't like to carry tales, but I'll ask you this, Harry. Do you know they say she's already carrying on with Dick Stewart?"

It's worked, I thought, just like I planned it. Only it's not the way I thought it would be.

Nothing is.

I stood up slowly and I made my voice flat and hard.

"I'll accept your apology," I said. "And I'll take the names of those who say it."

He looked at me and his eyes blinked once. I hated to make him feel the way he did because he was my friend. He looked smaller than he really was.

"You can have the apology. The best way to get the names is off the county tax lists. They ought to include about everybody."

"You better go, Brax. You better just get the hell out of here."

As I said it, we both heard the first sound of the Chevrolet. The sun was lowering now, and suddenly it was very hot there beneath the trees around the clear, silent spring. The air was still and the sounds of the car were projected ahead across the sand. It came over the low hill and we stood there and watched it.

"Why don't you ask her? You had bad luck with Lucy, Harry. I wouldn't want to see this one get you off the track again. Ask her now. Maybe there's nothing to it."

"No."

"Better find it out now."

"All right, then. And then you go. And don't come back."

He shrugged and flipped the cigar across the spring. We started walking slowly toward the car, now coming to a halt behind the shiny Buick. I towered over him and his head was down now, and I wanted to reach out and put my hand on his shoulder.

Good old Brax.

It had taken guts to tell me what he had, believing what he did, knowing only what he knew. It hadn't been any of his business. He could have let it go. But I was his friend and he had told me.

Jean was getting out of the car. She looked curiously at the little man beside me, whose head was bowed in worry and sorrow, and at my ramrod posture.

"Jean, this is Jordan. He used to be my lawyer."

"Howdy-do," Brax said.

"I've heard about you, Mr. Jordan."

"He talks too much," I said. "About things he ought to keep his mouth off of."

Her face wrinkled in a slight frown and she looked from me to him and back again. He said nothing.

"He says people talk. About you and Dick Stewart."

She took the cue without a hitch. I remembered again what a good actress she could be.

Fear flashed across her face and she took a step backward and her voice trembled.

"No," she said. "It's not so."

"You tell me. The truth. I'll believe you."

"I buy at his store. That's all. Honest, Harry!"

It was just right, the way she said it. No one would ever have believed her except a husband who worshiped her, who had made up his mind to believe her before she opened her mouth, a husband who would not hesitate to kill the man who proved her a liar.

"All right," I said. "That's good enough for me."

Brax turned away without a word. He got in the Buick and I thought again how the mass of it dwarfed him, the neat little man who had come out here to tell me what he thought I ought to know.

I stepped to the window of the Buick.

"You didn't say it, Brax. You just said they were talking."

He nodded and pressed the starter button. The smooth roar of the engine flooded the stillness.

"You let it be known," I said, "that it's not so."

"All right."

"And let it be known that I'll shoot the man that says it again."

"They ought to know that anyway," he said. And then the Buick pulled away and we stood there and watched it drop out of sight over the hill.

"That helps," she said.

"Yes. Only I hate to be so rough on him. He meant to be my friend."

"Maybe you shouldn't have been. We'll need him after we do it."

"I know Brax. You don't have to worry about him."

"He believes it, too. About me."

"That's the plan, isn't it?"

"Sure. Everybody thinks I'm a tramp."

"Well," I said, "it won't be much longer now."

Suddenly, I saw how tired she was. Not physically, perhaps, but from the strain of it, the thinking and the scheming, and the daily encounters with Stewart. Little lines crinkled at the corners of her eyes, and her movements as she turned toward the cabin were listless.

"You need to relax," I said. "It's getting on your nerves."

"It's enough to, isn't it?"

"Yes. More than enough. Let's go out tonight."

She stopped and looked back at me. She laughed harshly.

"Around here? Where? A corn-shucking?"

"Not the Stork Club. But there's a roadhouse the other side of St. Johns. The food's O.K. and there's a juke box. Lucy and I ... we used to go there sometimes. We could blow in some of your dough on a couple of steaks."

"I've never been to the Stork Club, anyway. You're on."

"Besides, we ought to get out some. People expect to see a man and his wife around. It'll make the whole thing more believable."

She moved closer and touched my arm.

"Just this once," she said, "let's don't mix business with pleasure."

"All right," I said. "Let's get started."

That was nine days after we were married.

In that time, she had cooked for me, washed my clothes, and scrubbed the shack until it shone. She had forced me to shave my heavy beard every day, to go into town and get a haircut; she had made me dress neatly, including tucking empty left sleeves into coat pockets or pinning them up, instead of letting them dangle, as I had done before.

My frame was already beginning to fill out from the good food and regular sleep that she saw to it that I had. And my muscles were hardening again, after the aching soreness of the first day or two.

Because she had made me work too. I had rigged up a pulley-rope attachment so that she could get water from the spring without going out of the house. Coming back from the haircut trip, I had brought with me an empty oil drum, and I had fashioned a tower for it and contrived a rude shower, like the ones we built overseas.

I had walled in the spring with clean pine lumber I had cut and shaped myself from the wooded area adjoining the Caldwell place, to keep out the crumbling sediment. I had even dug a deep hole for an outhouse and built a structure around it, again with lumber I had cut and sawed myself.

Inside the cabin I had built another rough chair and another bunk, across the floor from the first one, and I had replaced some of the weak floor planking and erected strong, new steps in place of the rickety old ones.

All of this I had done with one arm and with the old tool kit I had bought the day I had moved out there. I had worked and was growing strong again and I did not see the face any more now and I had taken down the stick upon which I used to hang the bean cans.

We rarely if ever mentioned the thing that lay at the bottom of both our minds. We avoided speaking of the day rushing closer and closer to us, of the irrevocable deed almost upon us. But I could see the pressure of it in her eyes and it must have been in mine, too.

For my part, the puzzle that had started in me that night on the floor of the shack continued to plague me. I had thought then, in almost blinding certainty, that I did not want to go through with it. Now I didn't know. I could still feel the cold rage pop in me at the thought of Dick Stewart and what he had done to Lucy, and the still unknown something he had known, learned, unearthed that had enabled him to do it. When I felt that, there would be no doubt in my mind.

But then would come the nights, the nights when we would lie in tortured determination, in a sort of suspended rigidity, waiting, waiting, breathless, for one of us to crack, to give in, to make the first move toward the other and that incredible impact of desire and despair and desperation.

And afterward (because one of us always did, one of us always made that first move) I would lie in the night and know again the almost unarguable truth of the love that I had been so sure of that first night when she had come to me. And know again too that my desire to kill Stewart was dead and gone, and that I would do it only for her.

Perhaps if she had seemed to return the feeling, we could together have found some solution. But she came to me in defeat, gave herself to me in despair, and left me in bitter and consuming shame. Had it been the same with me, there would have been no problem.

So, with this between us, and with the ever present, lurking, approaching moment always in our minds, it was no wonder we had both welcomed my idea of a night out. A little fun seemed a wonderful thing.

Maybe we could find it at the Lodge.

Chapter Sixteen

It was about a mile beyond St. Johns, a low, rambling concrete-block structure, with a parking lot between it and the highway. The front door opened into a small room with a counter at one side, lined with stools, and a few tables were scattered across the floor. Beyond this room a half wall, topped with dark green curtains, set off the main room.

We went on back, not looking at the few people in the front part, most of whom were men drinking beer, and paused in the doorway. It was a long, narrow room and a row of booths went along each side wall. The juke box was against the rear wall, between the two doors.

Willy Carson, a fat, balding party who managed to keep his whisky and beer sales not inside the law but not far enough outside to get the sheriff interested, had a sense of humor. You could tell it the minute you looked at those two doors, because each of them had a bird dog's head outlined on it in plywood and beneath one head was the word "Pointers" and beneath the other "Setters." That was the kind of place the Lodge was, and the kind of guy he was.

Willy was hurrying across the floor toward us now, and before he was within ten feet of me he was reaching for my hand.

"Harry! Am I glad to see you again! Boy, we missed you." He was pounding at my back now. "Just the other night I was saying now Harry's gone and got hisself married again, he better git to comin' out here some more. I was tellin' ..."

Willy was a harmless cuss and I was touched at his genuine welcome. I grinned back at him.

"Willy," I said, "this is Jean."

His eyes twinkled over fat cheeks and he grabbed her hand and began to pump it too. I cut

him off before he could go into the back-slapping
routine again.

"Got a booth for us, Willy?"

"Always got one for you, Harry. Right over by
the fan."

He led us to a booth near the rear. The place
wasn't more than half full. As we walked across the
floor, I could feel the other people there watching
us. I nodded at the ones I knew and they smiled
and waved. How the tongues will wag tomorrow, I
thought. They'll be telling all over the county about
that low-neck dress she's wearing.

We sat down and Willy oscillated over us.

"I got some good cold Miller's up there, Harry.
You always liked that Miller's."

I grinned at Jean.

"Bring her one, Willy. I'll have iced tea."

I could almost taste that beer. I could see the
thin head on it and feel it, cool and brash, in my
throat. But I ordered the iced tea anyway.

That had been the hardest thing of all. The
whisky.

I had stayed away from, it, and only then did I
realize the grip it had taken on me. In the nights I
ached for it and my head pounded for it, my dry
throat begged for it, and my nerves screamed for it.
But I had stayed away from it, and I did now, even
from a beer.

Because just one was all it would take. Just one
and I would never be rid of it again.

"Iced tea?" he said, his face screwed up in
bewilderment. "My God. I'll see if we got any."

"And bring us a couple of steaks, Willy. Some of
those good ones you always stick away for your
favorites. Make them rare. Plenty of French fries
and the other trimmings."

His face was happy again, then, and he toddled
off to put in the order.

"Well, this is it," I said. "The local hot spot."

She was looking around her, her face alive with interest. She had put on a dark cotton dress, and her tan shoulders and neck rose out of it to the small head and the eager face and the short blonde hair.

"I like it. It looks like these people have good times here."

"They do," I said, "because they only come here when they want to. They don't practically live here, like folks do in a big city."

"Maybe that's it. Harry, let's dance. I haven't danced since I left South America."

"All right. If you want to."

We got up and went back to the juke box and looked over the tunes. I dropped a nickel in.

"You pick it," I said.

She studied the list again and then punched "September Song."

I put my right arm around her waist. She rested her hand on my left shoulder, because there was no left hand.

After the first few halting steps nothing mattered. She was light as a feather. She put her head against me, just below the shoulder, and I felt the warm length of her against me, and suddenly, for those few moments, it was again as it was in the nights when we lay together in the shack and I looked at her while she slept.

Time vanished. The Lodge vanished. It all went away but the two of us, moving together on the worn dance floor, the slow sweet music only a dim and faraway ribbon between us.

Maybe it was because now I was feeling again the will in me to do anything and endure anything for her, even without the satisfaction of animal desire that had accompanied the feeling before. Or maybe it was like a plant growing in the land, like that one tiny absolute moment when the upward shoot of the plant breaks the last thin layer of earth and reaches for the air and the light.

Maybe that was such a moment. Because I thought, I know now. I know it as surely as I hold you in my arms. This is all I want now, just this and nothing else. This is all I want forever.

I felt her soft body moving against me.

God help me, I thought. I love you. I never meant to, but I do. No matter how it is with you, or what you do to me.

I love you.

And then it was over and we went slowly back to the booth, her hand in mine. Willy had the beer and the tea set out for us. We sat down and I smiled at her. And then I saw her lips were trembling.

"I didn't know my dancing was that bad."

She smiled a little and shook her head.

"I was just thinking. Everything could have been so different. I wish I'd been born in a place like this, instead of where I was. It might have been so different. But now ..."

"Hold it," I said. "No business tonight. Remember?"

"O.K. No business."

We sat there and talked a little, but not much. One or two people stopped by the table and I introduced her to them. Then Willy brought the steaks, sizzling on their hot platters, with huge mounds of French fries and cooked onions, and a special kind of slaw I never found anywhere except at his place, and a plate of hot biscuits.

She just reached over and cut up my steak in pieces, not too big, not too little.

When you eat one of Willy's steaks, you don't talk much. We sat there in silence, just eating, and when we had both finished, we looked at each other and laughed.

"I guess that shows up my cooking," she said.

"Think nothing of it. Willy's got a colored boy back in that kitchen who used to cook in a big resort hotel down at the beach. Willy has to get down on his knees every Saturday night and beg him to stay another week."

Just then I saw Lou Thomas get up from a booth across the room and start across the dance floor toward us. He's drunk, I thought. He's really plastered…

You had to know Lou to be able to tell that, because he could have a tankful on and only his eyes would reveal it. Lou ran an auto sales agency and he was all right most of the time, but he was a mean drunk. He was big and he was rough and when he was lit he was always looking for trouble.

He stopped at our booth and we both looked up at him.

"Hello, Lou."

"Harry. Want to dance with your wife."

His tongue was only a little thick, but his eyes were blurry and watering. That was the way you could tell it.

"You got a load on, Lou," I said, grinning at him, hoping he would let it pass and go away. "You might step on her or something."

"Let th' lady answer for h'self, why don' you?"

"I'll answer for her. She doesn't want to dance."

I felt my temper rising in me. I hate a mean drunk. If they can't hold it, they ought not to drink it.

Watery eyes narrowed. He leaned forward and put both hands on the table and then he looked right at her.

"They dared me," he said. "Said I didn't have th' nerve t'ask you to dance."

Lou didn't know her. He didn't know who he was dealing with. He hadn't picked on any bashful maiden this time. She leaned her head against the back of the booth and smiled faintly and ice dripped off each word.

"You've got your nerve, all right, mister. You've got plenty of nerve."

He straightened up abruptly and red moved down from his hair across his face.

"So I'm not good 'nough. Not like Dick Stewart. He's good 'nough, I reck'n."

I came up on my feet in one motion and out from behind the table in another and before he could move I hit him in the stomach, with all of me behind it. I felt my fist sink up to the wrist in his belly.

Stale whisky breath breezed over me and his mouth came open and he bent like a safety pin, his arms going across his stomach. I stepped back and reached out my hand to his shoulder and straightened him up.

Before he could flop over again I let him have it on die chin and he went over backward and lay there on the floor, the mouth open again and the head twisted over to the side.

I leaned over and took his shirt front in my hand and yanked his head off the floor. I was seeing red now and it felt good to know that I had been able to do it, that I still had the muscle and guts to do it. I stared into his face and the eyes were quite dull so I let his head fall back to the floor.

People were standing up now, and Willy was hurrying across the floor, his hands fluttering in protest. I swung around and looked at Jean. She hadn't moved and the little smile was frozen on her face.

"Let's get out of here," I said. She stood up obediently and I took her hand and we started for the door.

They were bending over Lou now and we had to push through them. I quieted Willy's bleats with a ten to cover the meal and then we were out of there and walking toward the car.

"He'll be all right," I said. "Whisky is a good shock absorber."

"I didn't mean for you to hit him."

"You just don't say things like that around here and not get hit."

"Well," she said. "I guess it turned out to be a business engagement after all."

"Yeah. I guess it did."

We hardly spoke on the way home that night. At first I felt almost lighthearted and gay.

For one thing, I knew that when I had hit Lou Thomas, I wasn't even thinking of the trail we were laying, of the way it would fit in with our plans. I had hit him out of pure, blinding rage at what he had said to her. I had fought for her and won and I was old-fashioned enough to feel good about that.

Sir Galahad, I thought. You and Sir Galahad.

For another thing, there was no longer any doubt in me that I loved her. Most of the puzzle had gone out of my head back there on the dance floor, and I could look at it straight and clear and know now that I loved her, had loved her since our wedding night on the floor of the shack.

But it all began to come home to me again as we neared the Old Caldwell place. Because my mind couldn't get away from the fact that we were going to kill a man. My gaiety went tumbling out the window of the old car.

If I didn't love her, I thought, if only that hadn't happened, I could get out of it. I could just go on and clear out and the hell with all of it. Or maybe not. Maybe this is my judgment for killing Lucy.

I turned my head and looked at her and saw that she was looking at me too, her eyes almost glowing in the night, and something turned inside of me, the same thing I had felt before, at the shack, back there in the Lodge. Something that not only left no doubt, but also not even the possibility that doubt existed.

So the door was closed behind me. The bridge was burned. Because, no matter how I felt, I would have to do it. I would have to help her, give her the thing that she thought would take away the pain and the hurt and the bitterness from inside of her, at the loss of something that to her had meant the very existence of—call it happiness.

Oh, I didn't fool myself. I knew what those nights in the cabin were for her. I knew I was merely something that had become necessary during the course of a larger, more important desire. I didn't fool myself.

But I would do it. And we would get away with it. And then?

What then, indeed?

We were digging his grave, all right. And we were digging a deep, hollow, clammy one for ourselves, right beside it.

Chapter Seventeen

She spent part of each day in town, laying her trail of unfaithfulness, which we knew now was becoming plain to all, to Brax Jordan and Lou Thomas and everyone who cared to think about it. She didn't miss a day at Stewart's, and at night she would tell me about it, of his increasing fear and hatred of her.

She went about her purpose with a single-minded, calm, and purposeful detachment. She seemed to take no pleasure in it. But she left each day with an air of determination and returned each night with a look of accomplishment. She was doing a job, a job she had to do, and one she could do well.

One night, to boost the cause, I had driven the Chevrolet into town and parked it in the alley behind Stewart's store. I stole away unseen, and slept in the woods near the edge of town. Before dawn, I went back and drove it away. That had been her idea, too.

She had others. Like the notes she would leave for him when she knew him to be out of the store, notes that contained innocuous remarks about the weather or some other general topic, but that were generously scented and entrusted to old Joe Buxton with an air of charming secrecy.

It was a good job, all right.

It was done with the finesse of an actress and the coldblooded skill of a scientist. By the time she decided it was time for me to go in to talk to Stewart, she had hung him in a frame tighter than a noose.

I parked the Chevrolet on the sun-baked street in front of the Coshocken General Mercantile Company, and I sat there a minute, studying the place and thinking it out before I went in and told him.

Then I got out and stepped into the cool shade of the old porch roof that fronted the store. Two men occupied the benches Stewart provided for his customers and their eyes were steady on me.

"John," I said. "Ben. How y'all?"

They nodded gravely. I stood ramrod straight and I looked at them steadily and made my eyes hard. I wanted to look like a man who had come on unpleasant business.

Ben spat a brown stream toward the curb and wiped his mouth with his hand. Then he removed the worn felt hat and ran his hand through his sandy red hair, thinning now, and replaced the hat.

"Don't see you around, Harry," he said.

"Fixing my place up. Haven't been in town much."

He nodded.

"Heerd you got married up," John said.

"That's right. Two weeks ago."

"I seen her. Right smart woman."

"Yes," I said.

John shifted his wad toward the other cheek. "Womenfolk is funny," he said. "Don't know why a man can't get on without 'em."

"I don't either," I said. "Or why he should want to."

They grinned, appreciating the joke, but there was no mirth in their eyes.

"Stewart in there?"

"I reckon. Leastways, he was a while ago."

I saw Ben's eyes go to my hip. What he was looking for was there, all right. I had taken the pistol out of the trunk again—the one that had killed Lucy, the one I had pointed at Stewart in this very store—and the bulge of it was plain in my pocket. I knew they were thinking what I wanted them to think: that I had come either to shoot Stewart or to give him fair and final warning.

I squared my shoulders and moved toward the store door.

"See you fellows," I said.

They nodded. I was aware of them, moving silently and easily as ghosts away from the porch, as I entered the store.

It was dim in there. Old Joe was seated at his desk in the rear, as he always was. I couldn't see any customers and the cool old leather and feed and fertilizer smell was there and little curls of dust puffed up from my feet as I walked slowly down the long floor toward the bookkeeper.

He looked up when I was halfway there and then watched me until I stood beside him. His eyes jumped in his thin skull.

"Hi, Joe," I said. "Stewart around?"

He nodded toward the little office, partitioned off at the back of the store.

"Set a spell, Harry," he said. "Don't see enough of you."

He said my name quite loudly and his uneasy glance swiveled from the office to me.

"I don't know," I said. "Like to talk, but I have to see Stewart."

"Harry ..." he said, and stopped, his upraised hand falling back to the desk.

"Yes."

He made a hopeless gesture with his hand. His face pleaded with me.

"He's back there."

"Thanks," I said. I moved a step or two away from him and then stopped and looked back.

"My wife comes in a lot, doesn't she?"

He jumped and blotted a paper in front of him with a drop of ink from the shaking pen.

"Why—er—I never noticed—er—no more than anybody. She buys a lot, I reckon."

"She doesn't buy much," I said. "But she comes in anyway, I reckon."

He didn't say anything and I grinned thinly at him and turned and walked on back to the door of Stewart's office.

I didn't knock. I pushed open the door and took two steps into the office and stopped. I felt him behind me.

"Don't you turn around," he said. "Don't you even move."

"All right," I said. "Take it easy, Dick."

"I'm not that big a fool," he said. "You know I wouldn't be that big a fool."

"I don't know," I said. "You can be right much of a jackass, time you set yourself to it."

"Not that big," he said. "I don't know what she's up to, but I haven't even smiled at her. Not once."

"I wouldn't worry about it," I said. "That's not why I'm here. Whatever it is you're talking about."

"I don't care why you're here," he said. "I want you out. And I don't want you back any more."

"I'm going to sit down in that chair," I said. "I reckon you have a gun on me, but if you shoot it you're going to get worse than I could ever give you."

I moved forward and sat down in the chair. In a moment I heard him take a step or two forward.

"You got trouble," I said. "All kinds of trouble."

He came into my range of vision then, moving carefully to my left, on my stump side, in a circle around me. Sweat was popping on his brow but the gun was very steady and straight, pointing at me.

"Put it down," I said. "I won't bite."

"What trouble? What trouble are you talking about?"

"Put it down," I said. "Then we can talk."

"All right. Take that gun out of your pocket and lay it down on the floor over here."

I grinned and reached into my pocket. He watched me narrowly and I saw his knuckles, white against the dark metal.

I put the pistol on the floor.

"Slide it this way," he said, and I did.

He kicked it with his toe into a corner of the room.

"That gun keeps popping up between us, doesn't it?" I said.

He didn't answer. He went around the corner of the desk and sat down in the big leather-covered chair and laid the pistol down on the dusty, paper-strewn desk. His hand hovered near it and the sweat was running freely on his face now.

"What trouble have I got?" he said.

I felt my teeth pull back in a grin I couldn't stop.

"This wife of mine," I said. "She's quite a bitch."

He just looked at me.

"She used to know Lucy."

His hands, twisting nervously in his lap, stopped, still and motionless, and his head jerked visibly, as if he had been slapped.

"Real well," I said. "They were old chums, you might say."

"All right," he choked. "So what?"

"So there were letters," I said. "A lot of letters. Like this one."

I reached inside my coat and pulled it out and tossed it on his desk. His hand reached for it, darting, and stopped just short of it. He licked his lips and suddenly his shoulders squared slightly and he picked it up and opened it and began to read.

I had worked so long to get it just right that I almost knew it from memory. I let the words of it run through my mind as I watched him read it. The first page was just routine stuff I had copied from one of the other letters. The real juice was in the last two paragraphs:

> You know I told you about this Dick Stewart in my last letter. I haven't told Harry anything about it yet. He would kill Stewart, I know he would, he has such an awful temper. Anyway, Stewart is coming out here tonight, or says he is, since Harry's away.

I don't know what I'll do. I'm in a
jam, Jean, and I don't know how to
get out of it. All I can do is just hope
and pray Harry never finds out.

It was a chance we had to take. But it stood to
reason, from what we knew of Lucy and of Stewart,
that she must have known he was coming that
night, that it was possible she would have written
such a letter. If she hadn't known he was coming—
well, it was a gamble.

I sat there and watched him while he read it.
Then he began to sag in the chair and I watched
his face break up and grow old under my eyes and
I laughed out loud.

"You see the date on that letter, don't you?" I
said.

"Yes."

"The day she died."

"Yes." He made an effort to get hold of himself.
"I don't believe she ever wrote this thing."

"That's all right. I don't care whether you
believe it or not. A jury probably would. By the
way, that's only a copy there. The real thing is safe
out at my place."

And then the gun was in his hand like lightning
and I looked at death in his eyes and in the shaking
hand.

"You shut up," he said. "I'm not going to take
any more. I'll kill you first."

I didn't say anything. There is a point beyond
which it is not safe to push even a rabbit. And he
was no rabbit. He was desperate, harried,
dangerous. I just sat there and watched him and
pretty soon the light went out of his eyes and he
put the gun down and I started to breathe again.

"All right," he said. "What are you going to do?"

I leaned forward slightly.

"I fixed it up that night," I said, "after you left it
all lying in my lap. I got us both off all right. Except

for a little matter of me being out one wife and one arm. But that letter could screw the works if the right people saw it."

He took another pull at the bottle.

"That's how she suckered me. I didn't know anything about her knowing Lucy until after she came out there and wiggled those hips at me and got me to marry her."

I stood up and walked around the desk and deliberately shoved the gun aside and sat down on the corner where it had been.

"She didn't know I didn't have any more money. She knew the farm was gone, but she thought I still had all the money I got for it and all the money I used to have, hid out somewhere. That was what she was interested in. She figured when she had me hitched up, fair and square, she'd spring the letter on me. There's enough in it to persuade the sheriff to open up the case again."

He listened as impassively as if I had been one of his customers, begging him to extend a little more credit.

"You see, she had it figured that I had found out somebody had been playing around with Lucy, but that I didn't know who. And that I had killed Lucy because of it, and then arranged the suicide. She thought the letter would force me to sign over all the money she thought I had to her. And she was pretty close to the truth, at that."

His face was a little puzzled now. He could feel it coming but he didn't know yet quite what shape it would take.

"She was real disappointed about my money," I said, "until I told her how it really happened that night, and about how much money your wife has."

"You bastard," he said. "You sonofabitch."

I grinned at him.

"So now you're going to play blackmail. Is that is?"

I shrugged. "Look at it this way. At the very least your wife would divorce you if that letter were

made public. You'd be out. Of course, I might go to
the chair. And you might go to jail. But what she's
interested in is the money, not you and me. I'd
rather just kill you and the hell with the money.
But she's not interested in that. So you see I've got
to play along with her, to save my own skin."

His fingers fumbled at a cigarette.

"The fair thing for you to do is to pay out a little
money," I said. "Not much. Not compared to what
it would cost you if your wife decided to boot you
out."

His sneer was an evil scar under his nose.

"The great Major London," he said. "The old
Southern gentleman. A common blackmailer."

My good arm swept out in a short, flat arc and
my open palm cracked across his cheek, then back,
and his head bobbed and the cigarette dropped
from his fingers. I took a handful of his shirt and
pulled him out of the chair and yanked him up close
to me.

"I could have killed you, Stewart. A hundred
times. I might do it yet. Slow and pretty. But I need
money now, I have a reason to need money again,
and you look like the Chase National Bank. You've
got to pay up to save my neck as well as your own.
But don't call me nasty names, lover boy. I have a
lot of reason to want to see you making worm food,
too. Don't ever forget that."

"Take your hands off me," he said, and I pushed
him in the chest, not gently, and he slumped back
in the chair. He looked at the gun and my face
dared him to pick it up.

He licked at his lips and I didn't laugh this time.
I just looked at him some more. A horn blew
furiously on the street outside and I heard the
faraway sound of the store door opening and
slamming shut and then the scrape of old Joe's
chair as he got up to wait on the customer.

"Twenty-five thousand dollars," I said. "That's
dirt cheap, even for both of our necks."

"When?" His voice was strangely quiet.

"Not all at once. We don't want to kill the goose that lays the golden eggs. You ought to be able to scrape up about five thousand in loose small bills here and there without your wife knowing."

He nodded. Suddenly there was no fear in his eyes, or hate, or anger. There was an intense nothingness there that I found vaguely disturbing. My voice dropped and I hitched closer to him.

"Friday night," I said. "You can get that much by then."

He nodded again.

"That'll do for a starter. Six months from then we'll need five more. And so on till we get the whole shebang."

"I don't have any choice," he said. "Where do I pay off Friday?"

"At my place." He convinced damned easy, I thought. He folded up the minute I swung a hand in his face. Contempt for him curled my insides and for a moment I took all the old pleasure in the thought of how it was going to be for him.

Just for a moment.

"All right. When do I get the letter?"

"When we get all the twenty-five thousand." A shadow creased across his face. "But we're giving you some insurance. When you make the first payment we skip out of this burg. We're going to sell her car and you can drive us from my place over to Belleview to catch a train, just so you'll know we've left. Then we'll get in touch with you about the rest of the money."

"All right. Now get out."

"I'm going. Listen, what was that crap you were giving me about Jean when I came in? Has she been putting the make on you?"

He flinched. "You keep her out of here," he said. "She ought to have better sense."

I laughed. "If you don't beat all. Good thing I'm not in love with this one. I'd have to call this deal off and blow a hole in you. Like I ought to do anyway."

"I haven't touched her. She just hangs around all the time."

"I bet you haven't. That girl wouldn't be hanging around here for nothing, and I've had a sample of your attitude toward other people's wives. I wondered what she spent so much time in town for. Like I said, it's a good thing she isn't Lucy."

I walked over to the corner, picked up my gun, and put it in my pocket. Then I started out the door.

"Harry," he said.

I stopped and looked over my shoulder at him.

"Suppose I don't pay. If you use that letter everybody will know about me and Lucy."

"That's right."

"You never had the guts to risk that before. Maybe you don't now. Maybe I ought to tell you to go to hell."

I threw back my head and laughed.

"I'm in it because I have to be," I said. "I told you that. That girl's got us both over a barrel, Stewart. And she wouldn't mind kicking hell out of us both, if she doesn't get the money. You might remember that, if you get tempted to try some funny business."

I studied him carefully. He had grown calm, too calm. It wasn't like him. Maybe you get to the point, I thought, where you can't be anything else but calm. Maybe there just isn't any use in being anything else.

"All right," I said. "Better make it about nine Friday night, so we can catch that train in Belleview."

"I'll be there," he said. "I'll pay. But there's one thing you won't get from me, Harry. You won't ever get it."

"What?"

"What you'd really like to know. Whether what happened between Lucy and me was my fault or hers. How I really came to be there that night. You won't ever get that from me."

"Just bring the money," I said. "That's all I want from you now."

I opened the door and went on out, past old Joe, back at his desk now, and out of the store and into the old Chevrolet. I drove slowly out of St. Johns and then I hit open country and mashed harder on the pedal.

He was right. He was the only person alive who knew what had really happened between him and Lucy. I would never know. The secret would die with him.

Friday night.

And I wanted to know. I needed to know.

Not because I was still carrying the torch for her, not because I did not already know that it hadn't been a betrayal of me. Both of those reasons had gone with Jean, in the way I had come to feel for her and in the things she had told me of Lucy, in the letters she had shown me.

No. It was because, and I did not deny it even to myself, I needed to hear him admit it. I needed to hear the words come through his lips, saying:

"She loved you. She only went with me, not to betray you, but to save you, save you from hurt and disillusionment. Lucy never betrayed you."

I already knew it. But I needed to hear him admit it. And I never would.

I put the gas pedal to the floorboard and the old car leaped and sped on down the road.

Chapter Eighteen

She was standing in the door of the cabin, her thumbs hooked in the waistband of the same slacks she had worn that first day. I got out of the car and walked across the sand toward her.

"When?" she asked. I could see her jaws tighten when I said:

"Friday."

"Good."

She stood aside and I went on in the house and sat down on the bunk. She didn't take her eyes from me. Her hands moved nervously at her waist.

"You want it to be over too," I said. "You're jumpy as a cat."

"Yes. I want it to be over. Who wouldn't?"

"You went in with your eyes open, didn't you?"

Her voice flared at me. "You don't look so happy yourself."

I looked at her steadily and I meant every word I said.

"I wish I'd never laid eyes on you, Jean."

She didn't say anything to that. I do, I thought, I wish I'd never seen you. But if I hadn't, if I hadn't found you, I would still be just a cadaver, just a breathing corpse, aimless, gutless, lifeless. I don't know.

"I should have just shot him," I said, "right out in the open. I should have had the guts. That's what I ought to have done."

"Nerves," she said. "Just nerves. That's your whole trouble."

"You're a fine one to talk."

We didn't say anything for a long time. Then I began to tell her about Stewart, and the talk we had had, leaving out what he had said about Lucy.

"And now he's hooked," I said. "Everything is all set up."

She came over and sat on the bunk by me and suddenly I was very conscious of the scent of her and the warmth of her leg along mine. I felt her hands on the muscle of my arm.

"You're strong again," she said.

I didn't look at her.

"Your face has filled out and your eyes are clear. I can feel the strength in you. All the strength of two arms in this one."

"I feel a lot better," I said.

"You haven't had a drink since we were married and you're clean again."

I laughed. "As the driven snow," I said. "Just like a baby's breath."

"When we do it you'll be all whole again. You'll be the man you used to be again. You'll get it all out of you."

I felt her hands moving on my chest now, and then they fumbled at the buttons of my shirt. Her fingers were cool and tingling on the skin of my chest and stomach. I felt her breath against my ear and her lips were hot on the back of my neck.

I didn't move. All my shirt buttons were open now, and I heard her whisper: "Don't think about it, Harry. Think about me."

I stood up then and pushed her hands roughly away and walked to the other side of the room. I stood there buttoning my shirt, and I could hear her breathe a little harder.

"You don't have to throw me any more bones," I said. "I'm going to do it. It was my idea, remember?"

"I wasn't …"

I spun around and almost yelled at her.

"All that nonsense!" I said. "About how strong I am. You were afraid I'd back out on you. So you thought you had to nerve me up a little, give me another little piece to urge me on. As if you hadn't given me enough already. Well, you can keep it, sister, from now on. I don't want it, not that way! Not any more."

"You're wrong," she said. "You're all wrong."

"Maybe I am. Maybe not. But don't worry about my backing out."

There was a sick hurt in me for her to have been so obvious and raw about it. Somehow in the harsh daylight it seemed obscene and incredibly evil that she should sway her body against me to ensure that I would kill a man. It had not seemed so in the moonlight, in the soft and sighing night.

Why did I have to fall in love with the bitch? I thought. Why couldn't it have been some simple uncomplicated girl with a home and babies on her mind, no thought of killing anybody or even hating anybody? What did she do to me that made me forget the ugly cancer between us and the reason behind her kisses and the thing she wanted from me all along?

"I'm sorry you feel like that about me, Harry."

"All right," I said. "Just let it go, will you?"

She got up and walked steadily past me, out the door and on across the sand, and then she disappeared beyond the big dune. I went to the door and stood looking after her, and I never loved her so much as then. Because the lonely slump of her shoulders and the defeated way she walked told me what it was that made me love her. Not the nights, not the bodies entwined in passion, but the deep hurt and loneliness in her, the complete absence of hope, not bitterness, not anger, just final and irrevocable hopelessness.

That was the thing in her that something in me answered, could not forget or ignore. That was the thing Dick Stewart had brought to her, and that was the thing she thought I alone, and what I would do, could ease.

You poor kid, I thought. You haven't got a chance.

My trip to see Stewart finished my part of it, except for one more little thing. I dreaded it, because after the talk we had had the other day, it was going to be hard to face Brax Jordan.

But it had to be done. I had been in to see Stewart on Tuesday and set up the works for Friday night. So on Thursday morning, bright and early, I hopped in the old Chevrolet again and headed back to St. Johns.

Brax kept an office on the second floor of a ramshackle building that housed a barbershop and a poolroom. It wasn't much of a building, but it was right in the center of town and Brax had always loved pool. He was the local champion.

I closed the door behind me and leaned back against it and looked at him. He paused in his work, then took the spectacles from his nose and leaned back in the leather swivel chair. His face and eyes were quite blank and the cigar stub in his mouth was dead and unburning.

"You were right," I said.

He said nothing. He took the cigar stub from his mouth and tossed it across the desk to the floor. I almost grinned, it was such a familiar gesture. He kept no ash tray in his office, and the floor was burned and scarred in hundreds of spots where he had thrown still burning butts.

But I kept the grin off my face. I was playing a part and my neck and hers could depend on it. Brax Jordan was my friend, but he was smart too, and he was honest, and he would be the first to turn us in if he found out what the game was.

We would need him, the best lawyer in the eastern part of the state, after Friday night. I was gambling that he would do it, that he would go along with us, but I knew that if he knew the real scheme, including her part of it, he would never touch it.

"I'm going to kill the bastard," I said.

He grunted.

"And you want me to get you off for it," he said.

I moved away from the door and sat down in his visitor's chair.

"You got me to thinking," I said. "I kept an eye on her. And I found out it's true."

"When are you going to do it?"

"The next time I catch them together."

He snorted. "You ought not to have told me. That makes it premeditation."

"They won't convict me for doing it. Not if I catch him with her."

"No. And not if I defend you. I could get you off, all right. The unwritten law hasn't ever been repealed in these parts. But premeditation makes it different."

"The hell with premeditation. You can forget I was here."

He nodded and put the glasses back on his nose.

"I could. If I was going to defend you."

That stopped me. I hadn't expected that from him.

He leaned farther back in the chair and put his hands behind his head and his owl eyes bored into me.

"I stood by," he said, "and let you sell off the best farm in this county and the house you and your dad were born in and your mother died in. I even helped you do it. I was a big enough damn fool to give away all your money for you. And all of that for a Yankee girl who killed herself and tried to kill you too. Sometimes I wish she hadn't been such a lousy shot."

I sat forward in my chair and opened my mouth to speak, but his upraised hand stopped me.

"I've been too lenient with you for too long now. After all that I just mentioned, I let you make an ass out of yourself and a drunken bum to boot for two solid damn years, and when some chippie comes along and grabs you off, for some ungodly reason the Lord Himself couldn't figure out, I even tried to overlook that too."

"You better shut up," I said. The little bastard, I thought, I never saw him so mad before. If I lifted a hand he'd come flying over that desk at me like a fighting cock.

"And now you have the colossal gall—and after I warned you what was coming and you ran me off what you call your place—to walk in here and tell me you're deliberately planning to murder a man for seducing this chippie and ask me to get you off from the electric chair, which is the best place I can think of for a bird-brain like you."

"All right," I said, standing up. "If that's the way you feel about it, I can't help it." How can I get him to come around? I wondered. I never figured this, that premeditation angle. If he wants to, he can get me fried now. He's got to come around.

"Sit down," he said. "I'm not through with you yet."

I stood looking at him, my arm hanging motionless at my side, my empty left sleeve neatly tucked in my coat pocket.

"I never broke the law in my life," he said. "I have too much respect for it. At least I had, up until you went haywire."

He swung himself forward and his short legs dangled and then his feet touched the floor and he got up and went over to the big old safe standing open in the corner. He knelt down and took out a big envelope, bound with a rubber band.

"That's the worst thing I let you do to me," he said. "I broke the law for you."

He had me genuinely puzzled now. "I don't get it, Brax."

"I disposed of your holdings," he said, "and I gave all the money to the polio foundation. Only I juggled the books around a little bit and held out this. Ten thousand dollars."

He tossed the envelope at me and I caught it and looked inside. I didn't count it, but I knew there was at least that much there.

"I could have gone to jail for that, because I knew if I asked your permission you'd say no, and so I had to fix it up so there wasn't any record of it.

That's why it's in cash. You don't even have to pay tax on it."

"I still don't understand."

"You wouldn't. But maybe I can spell it out for you. There's enough there for you to catch the first train out of here and go about a thousand miles away from here and settle down somewhere and forget all this and get started again. Buy one of those artificial arms. There's nothing here to hold you."

"Except Stewart."

"Not even him. Because all he's done is grab that girl away from you and you never had her long enough to worry about that, if you use a little common sense about it. Which is, I suppose, asking a lot of you."

"I could just take the money," I said. "It's mine."

"No. Because I've got those bills numbered and I can prove you stole them from me if I want to. If I juggled them out of your accounts I can sure-God juggle them right into mine, any time I feel like it. You couldn't, but I could."

"All right. I believe you." I tossed the envelope back across the desk to him. "That's your fee. For defending me for shooting Dick Stewart."

"I'll be goddamned," he said, and flopped back in the chair again.

"Listen," I said. "I never asked much out of life. But what I had, what I wanted most, was Lucy, and the Lord took her away from me. He took my arm away from me too. And now I've found something else I want, something I thought could make up for Lucy and for my arm, and now Stewart's taken her away from me. I couldn't do anything about the Lord, but I can about him, and I'm going to."

I felt cheap saying it; I felt dirty and treacherous. Because I knew I was deliberately trying to get him to do it for her; I was playing on the friendship and affection I knew he had for me to save her neck. Because if it was just my neck, I wouldn't be planning to risk it any more. I was risking mine for her and I was asking him to go against all his principles for her. I was using the grimy trick of arousing his pity to get him to do it.

I couldn't look at him then and I got up and turned my back to the big desk and looked out the window at the desolate, sun-swept street below.

For a long time he didn't say anything and the silence in the office grew thick and miasmic and I felt it coming up off the rug and choking me. Why doesn't he say something? I thought. Why doesn't he just go on and tell me to get the hell out or something, not just sit there and keep me sweating like a field hand picking cotton?

"All right," he said, his voice dull and flat. "If you do it, I'll get you off. On one condition."

"Name it." I was facing him now, but I still did not meet his gaze.

"When it's done, you take this money and get out of here, like I said, and make something out of yourself again."

"What about her?"

He laughed, short and sharp.

"If you're going to kill a man for her, I don't expect you to toss her out. Not you."

"All right. I'll do it."

"Listen, Harry. I know how you feel. I can imagine if it were my wife. But it won't help any. Murder never helped anybody."

"I have to do it, Brax. It's like I can't help myself."

I almost gagged on the words.

"All right. I know you have to do it. Now get out of here. Just go on and leave me alone."

I walked out and on down the stairs. I didn't thank him. That would have been the final blow, because I knew he was also just doing what he had to do, what his whole life as an honorable man who stood by his friends had forced him to do. I didn't thank him for throwing aside everything else that same life had taught him for that principle of standing by a friend.

So now it was all ready, the trap was set, the trigger was ready to be pulled. We had laid a trail of lies and deception. I would shoot him and then we would go to court and the man I had pulled into our scheme of deceit and death would swear with us that what we had done was justifiable in the sight of God and we would go free.

And I didn't even want to do it any more. Maybe I never really had. But I would do it, and I would draw him into it with me, because it was what she wanted and, God help me, it was what I meant for her to have.

Chapter Nineteen

The sun was already beginning to sink in the sky when I drove the Chevrolet out of the rutted road that led from our little shack out through the trees to the bigger road. Instead of turning right when I reached that road and driving on to the paved highway that led into St. Johns, I wheeled the car to the left.

The dirt road upon which I drove was a connection between the highway through St. Johns and another paved highway that led into Belleview, a much larger town, about thirty miles away in an adjoining county. From the shack to the Belleview highway, it was about eight miles.

The road was seldom traveled, for it ran through the poorest farm region of the county and only one or two small houses were located along it. The dairy truck came by each morning, and a few mule wagons and an occasional car moved over it in the daytime. But at night, any vehicle was a rarity on that road. That was what made it the perfect place for what we had in mind.

I had the spot picked out. It was only about a half mile from the end of the road, where it joined the Belleview highway. At that junction was a filling station and store where there was a telephone. That would make it easy to get in touch with the Sheriff.

I drove slowly along the washboard road. We had had no rain in some time and yellow clouds of dust mushroomed behind the Chevrolet. The sky was bright blue and the sun was hot and blazing. Soon my hand on the wheel was gritty with the sweat and the dust.

In about twenty minutes I came to the place I was looking for and braked the Chevrolet to a stop. There was a small road leading off into the woods, a lonely, secret slash in the pines, even less defined than the ruts leading into my place.

An old signboard, nailed to a tree, slanted at a crazy angle. The weather had beaten hard against it, but I could still trace the faint, disappearing letters: "Rutherford Mill."

It had not been used in years. The mill building itself had long ago collapsed and disintegrated, and only a few rotting scraps of lumber among the weeds and the old stone foundation remembered its existence. The huge old wheel had vanished, too, but the pond was still there, deep and black and treacherous, and the dark waters still dropped over the stone spillway to the anonymous little creek that wound its way to the river.

The little road I looked at now led to that pond and what had been the old mill, only a few hundred yards away beyond the thick screen of pines.

I peered at the road and saw tire tracks entering it, not new and not just one car, but the sort of tracks a few cars, passing occasionally, will leave.

That bothered me. I hadn't thought the road would be used.

All I need is for somebody to have a still going down there, I thought. That would make everything just ducky. Like a hole in the head.

I stepped down on the gas again and the car nosed into the old road. It was not hard going, although a few branches banged against the windshield and gnarled old roots poked through the earth to jolt against the tires.

In a few minutes I came out of the trees and onto the shore of the pond. Along that part of the lake the former mill owners had erected a stone dam, so that the water was deep right up to the edge. On the far side of the lake a small beach backed up against the forest.

I cut the engine and the sound of it faded into the silence. I sat there a moment looking out across the still water. It was pocked and scarred with jagged stumps, rising starkly out of the water, and the surface of it was black, and you got a sense of the evil depths lurking beneath those stumps and that calm, still surface, and of the power of all that water contained there, waiting there. From far to my right the rush of the water over the small spillway carried faintly to me.

I shuddered, looking at it. I thought about the bodies that had disappeared under that even sheen of evil, broken only by the stumps, because under that sheen tangling vines and weeds and water-thriving growth waited, reached, to choke around the legs and the waists and the arms of people who swam there.

The pond had long ago been outlawed for swimming, but that didn't stop it. There are always fools, and every summer somebody drowned in Rutherford Millpond. Sometimes they recovered the body and sometimes they didn't. Few people cared to dive down to search for a drowned body in that lake.

Then I remembered the tire tracks and the worry went out of me about that. I looked out at the strip of sand running up to the dam, and sure enough, the tracks were there too.

Probably kids, I thought. Swimming out here at night. The fools. Let them just stay away tonight.

I looked again at the water. A good place to kill a man, I thought, especially if you have to get rid of the body. We don't have to do that, but it's a good place anyway.

I cranked up the engine again and pulled the car over to the side of the road that led into the pines. I cut the switch and got out and stood there a minute, thinking it all over, looking hard for anything we had done wrong, anything we had missed.

I couldn't find a thing. It had all worked out perfectly. Just the way I had planned it. Yeah, I thought. You're so goddamn smart. Harry London, Ph.D., Phi Beta Kappa, S-A-P.

I kicked at one of the tires and then I walked back along the silent road to the bigger one that lay, dusty and long, between me and the old Caldwell place. The sun was very low now and I did not think I would be seen. I could work through the woods around the few houses or duck off the road if I spotted anyone coming and still be home long before nine.

I would be there in time, all right. And she would be waiting for me, with the pistol ready.

It was good dark now, and the sky was brilliant with stars. There would be a moon later, not a full one, but in the night it would hang above us like an all-seeing eye, and I thought that whatever we did, whatever happened, the moon would know the truth.

And wherever you go, you can't get away from the moon.

Crickets dinned all about me and a night bird sang sweetly. The tall pines cast shadows over the road, and along its edge, where I walked, it was very dark.

I was nearly there now, almost to the road leading into the shack, and then I saw something move under a tree. I stopped very still and watched.

Then she stepped out into the road and the stars spilled their light across her.

She was dressed very simply, in a white dress I had not seen before and high heels. The starlight, mellow and pale on her face, took all the faint traces of hardness from it, and she looked no more than sixteen. I took a step toward her and realized again that the top of her head did not come even to my shoulders.

"You took so long," she said.

I was moved by a sudden urge to put my arm around her, to feel the close blonde hair against my face, and the surge of her against me, and the warm, soft lips, and I almost reached for her.

Then I remembered what lay ahead for us, waiting in the night.

"Did you think I wasn't coming back?" I said. My voice was more harsh than I had meant it to be.

"No. I was just afraid something had gone wrong."

"I'll bet you were," I said. "I'll bet that scared you to death."

I started walking on and she turned and fell in beside me. We entered the narrow road through the scrub in silence. I didn't slow my pace. She had to hurry to keep up and I saw that the skirt of the white dress was slim and binding on her legs and I slowed down.

"That's a fine getup for the glorious occasion," I said. "Maybe we could paint a skull and crossbones across the bosom."

"That isn't funny."

"No. But then, I didn't mean it to be."

"I would be pretty well dressed," she said. "If it actually was the way we're going to make it look, I mean."

"All right," I said. "Don't expect me to pay the dry cleaner's bill. It costs a lot to get blood out of white cloth."

She didn't answer that. Far ahead of us now I could see the dim patch of light that marked the spot where the road entered the sand. The trees around us were not so tall as those out by the bigger road, but their shadows cast eerie patches of dark ahead of us.

"You've got it all straight, I hope," I said. "You'd better not miss a trick or you're going to find yourself sitting in a chair you won't ever get out of again."

"I know what to do," she said. "My part's not hard any more. It's you that can't make any mistakes now."

"I won't," I said. "When we get almost to that road, I put the gun in his neck and tell him to stop.

Then you drive and we turn into the little road and go down to the lake. Then ..."

"Yes. Then you do it."

"Then I do it," I said. "And then I muss you up a little, like I'd slapped you around some, and we get in your car and drive to that little filling station on the highway. We call the Sheriff and I tell him I caught you and Stewart engaging in a spot of sexual intercourse and deceased him on the spot."

"That isn't funny either."

"Nothing's funny," I said. "I told you that once."

Suddenly it came to me that she was speaking in a small voice, almost shaky, and that she had not once barked back at me when I snapped at her. It's getting to her now, I thought. It's getting close and she's not so cold-blooded about it now.

I didn't want to make any more bright remarks then. There was no use in riding her.

"The part after will be tough," I said. "That'll be worse on you than on me. They'll crucify you and say how they don't blame me a bit."

"I know. I almost wish we were going to bury him somewhere and just go off and hope they never found him."

"Uh-uh," I said. "Not on your life. We'd spend the rest of our lives getting hives every time we saw a traffic cop. We'd be afraid to show our faces anywhere. It's better this way. We go on trial, we tell our story, and we get acquitted. Brax Jordan will get us acquitted. Then it's over and we don't have to worry about it any more."

Big talk, I thought. Mighty big. Mighty empty. Neither of us will ever think of anything else after tonight.

Then we were out from under the trees and walking across the sand toward the last big dune that hid the shack from us.

"How about the cabin? Is it all fixed?"

"I don't know. I did my best."

"When Stewart comes, it's got to look to him as if we're leaving. But only because he thinks we are, anyway. It can't look that way to anybody else."

"I've got a couple of bags of sand in each of those old suitcases of mine. They'll fool him. You can sink them in that lake—after you do it."

"That sounds good. That ought to take care of it."

We came over the rise and the kerosene glow from the door of the shack was surprisingly cheerful and welcoming across the brilliant night.

"Just a cottage small by a waterfall," I said. "But we call it home."

"It's all right. You don't need a big house. You can be happy even in a place like this, if you have to."

"Not us," I said. "We've got to play God. Who ever heard of God living in a shack?"

I stood back and let her go in first. The bags were standing by the bunk and the room had a stripped look. She had achieved it by hiding away a few things, things Stewart might reasonably expect us to carry along, but leaving out a few things too, so that if anybody cared to look we could still claim we had never planned to leave.

She stood in the middle of the floor, her hands clasped together. Then she turned her head and looked at me over her shoulder.

"Now what?"

"Now we wait," I said. "He ought to be along any time now."

They say when you are dying—drowning, for instance—all of your life passes in review before your mind's unwinking eye, a sort of monstrous omniscient newsreel of memory flickering across a giant screen to outline in relentless light all the things you could have been, might have done, should have achieved if it hadn't been for all the things you actually had been and done and achieved.

It is no different when you have elected yourself
God's agent and are waiting to kill a man. Only if
you have the guts and the luck and the strength,
you can then get up and walk out of the theatre and
give God back the franchise He never meant for
you to have anyway and start trying to make up for
all that the newsreel has hurled at you out of your
own blindness.

I could walk out of it, I was thinking as we sat
there and waited for the sound of his car, I could
still get out of it. If I could only make her see, if I
could only get her out of it too. If I could only be
sure she wouldn't go on and do it anyway and get
herself electrocuted.

Then I remembered her voice, the shaky little
inflection and the stillness of it, and I thought,
Maybe I can.

She sat calmly on the bunk, her feet in the high-
heeled shoes placed together and her knees
together too under the white skirt, her hands
quietly folded in her lap, the thin shoulders bent a
little, and her eyes steadily focused on nothing.

I love her, I thought. There isn't any sense to it,
no rhyme, no reason, no logic, but I do. Because she
has in her the same dead hopelessness I once
carried in me. Because she delivered me from it.
Because—yes, by God!—because I could deliver her
from it if she'd let me.

I could give her hope again. I could show her
that there is a place for her, that she can find
security and love and whatever all the things are
that add up to happiness.

But not if we do this thing. Not ever then.

I have to try. I can't let her do it without trying.

"Jean," I said.

She lifted her head and looked at me.

"I don't want to do it."

Faint puzzlement knitted her brows.

"I don't want you to do it either. I want us to
clear out of here now."

"I don't understand."

"Don't you see? Murder—it doesn't end anything. Do you think you'll ever sleep again at night? Do you think you'll ever feel any better than you do right this minute *after* we've done it? We've been wrong, Jean, so wrong, all down the line."

She began to laugh. Her head went back and her mouth opened and her laughter rang out across the room and into the night and bounced back at us from the dunes. She fell back against the wall of the cabin and her hands waved helplessly in front of her and peal after peal of terrible laughter came tumbling from her throat.

I sat there and watched her and my thoughts were bitter. All right, I thought, so it's no use. So it just makes her laugh. I'm going to tell it to her anyway.

She had quieted a little now and I went over and put my hand on her shoulder.

"That night," I said, "that night after we were married—and all the others—I knew then I didn't want to kill him any more. I would have told you a long time ago. But I thought you'd go on and do it by yourself if I backed out of it. I thought nothing would stop you."

"So now you tell me."

"I had to. I had to make a try at stopping it."

"Why didn't you do it sooner? Why didn't you tell me?"

"Damnit, can't you see why? I love you, Jean. If you're going to go through with it, I'll help you. I've got to help you. But I don't want to any more, and I don't want you to, either."

"You fool," she said. "Oh, you stinking, blind fool! You thought *I* wanted to do it! You were doing it for *me!* Oh, Harry, you fool ... you fool...."

She began to laugh again and I watched her. And then I knew. I knew how right she was and what a fool I'd been.

What fools we'd both been.

I laughed, too. It began to come plunging out of me, out of my belly, and I couldn't stop it. I sat down on the bunk beside her and put my arm around her and she clung to me. We rocked back and forth together and our wild helpless laughter rang through the cabin and out into the night. We couldn't quit and we began to ache from it and still we laughed, and only his voice stopped us:

"Somebody tell me the joke. Maybe I can laugh too."

Chapter Twenty

Even then, we couldn't stop it, not altogether, not all at once, not even looking down the barrel of his pistol.

He stood there, not moving, the pistol quite steady, and slowly it all went out of us and we sat there, clutched together, watching him, not laughing any more.

"Maybe you were laughing at me," he said. "Maybe you were thinking what a gag it is to blackmail a man."

I felt her grip tighten suddenly on me and then I slowly stood up and I felt her reluctant hands let me go.

"It's all off," I said. "You can put that thing down and go home. You can forget about it."

"Forget about it, eh?"

"Yes," I said. "You wouldn't believe why, if I told you. But we aren't going to bother you any more."

"You aren't going to bother anybody any more. Not ever."

It began to dawn on me then what he meant to do. And I knew, suddenly, the thing we had forgotten.

"You had it all figured, didn't you?" he said. "You'd bleed me white and I couldn't do anything about it. Only you got careless."

"Not careless. I tell you, we just called the whole thing off."

He laughed.

"You just called off twenty-five thousand dollars? Like that? Don't make me laugh."

It would happen this way, I thought, just when we both quit being fools, just when we both found out we didn't want any part of it, when we had a chance to get out from under it, it would have to happen, the one thing we didn't think of: that he might decide to fight back, that he too might plan murder.

Jean stood up beside me and I saw in her face that she had figured it out, too.

"Give him the letters," I said. "The real ones. Let him have them. There's nothing in them, anyway."

I can't let him find out, I thought. If he tumbles to what we really had in mind, he'll never believe we backed out of that one too. He'll think he has to do it, just to stay alive. We've got to keep him from finding out.

"They're in my pocketbook," she said.

He frowned a little, worriedly, and hope leaped in me. He moved cautiously to the shelf where the pocketbook lay and took out the packet of letters. The gun still pointed steadily at me. He glanced at them in quick takes, never letting his eyes drop from us long enough for me to jump him.

It took him a long time to finish them. Finally, he dropped them carelessly to the floor.

"I can't figure it. What the hell's going on? What about the one you showed me?"

"It was a fake. We were bluffing. We thought we could pull it off and collect a little cash. Then just tonight we got cold feet and decided to call it off. I swear it."

He's got to swallow it. It can't all end this way, just when everything should be beginning. It can't!

His face was creased in a frown now, his head cocked to one side, the gun still covering us. I could feel sweat beginning to prickle all over me.

I took a good look at his flushed face and I saw him shift his feet and it came to me in a flash that he had been drinking. He's had to nerve himself up, I thought.

He was thinking hard now, and suddenly he snapped his fingers, the pop loud in the hot silence, and my stomach began to curl up.

"So that's why you kept throwing yourself at me," he said, his eyes darting at Jean.

"I don't know what you're talking about."

"You got half the county talking about us, haven't you, and I never laid a finger on you."

Neither of us said anything, and he grinned, slowly and evilly.

"You're smarter than I thought," he said. "You were going to shoot me and plead the unwritten law. The blackmail talk was just to get me out here alone with you."

It was all over. I knew it now. He had figured it right, the one thing he could have done to make himself absolutely sure he had to kill us.

"All right, Stewart. That was it. But we gave that up, too. We got cold feet, like I told you. We were going to call it off."

His laugh was a dry, harsh rattle.

"Go on," he said. "Beg me. You had me begging once, Harry. Now it's your turn."

"What's the use? Your mind's made up."

He laughed again.

"That's right. My mind's made up."

He began to back away, still covering us, until he was standing almost in the door. Then he bent his knees slowly and picked up a coil of rope.

I hadn't seen it before. He shook it out and there was already a loop in one end of it, tied with a slipknot. He carefully dropped the loop to the floor and spread it out with his toe. He let the rope run through his fingers until his free hand held the other end of it.

"All right," he said. "Stretch out on the floor, Harry, and put your arm in that loop."

I shook my head.

"You'll have to do it without that," I said. "If you shoot us, I'll be damned if I'll let you work whatever scheme you've got. You'll have to shoot us here, where we stand."

He laughed.

"Listen, you don't think I came out here without an alibi, do you? You don't think anybody's ever going to connect me with you two disappearing, do you? Because I don't think you'll ever be even found, whether I shoot you here or anywhere else. Not the way I'm going to fix it. It'll be safer for me if you co-operate. But you're going to get it, either way."

I thought fast. You could see in the flushed face and the burning eyes that he meant it. And of course, he would have to have a plan. He would have foreseen some such argument as I had put up, and besides that, every minute I could just stay alive would give me another moment when I might have a chance to jump him.

I lay down on the floor and stretched my arm into the loop.

"That's a good boy," he said. "Now you." The pistol moved toward Jean. "Both of your arms."

She lay down beside me and put her arms out into the loop. I took one of her hands and felt her squeeze back.

He jerked the rope and the loop slipped tight around all three arms.

"Now get up."

Slowly, unable to use our arms, we clambered to our feet. He pulled the loop tighter around our forearms. That pulled us around face to face and I looked down at her and tried to smile.

"Maybe this is what we get," I said. "Maybe this is what we should have expected all along." I kissed her forehead.

"Isn't that sweet?" Stewart said. "Wait a minute, Harry, and I'll get her up close."

I glared at him and he laughed. He snapped the rope over our heads a couple of times, pulling us tighter together. Then he walked around and around us until the rope bound us securely together, from our shoulders down to our waists. We could move only our hands and our feet.

Still pulling the rope tight, he slipped the pistol in his waistband and came up behind her and fastened the loose end securely through one of the loops around her.

"Now," he said. "Move toward the door."

We had to take short side steps to walk at all, but we finally got there. When we stood right at the door sill he reached out both arms and pushed us sprawling through the door and down the steps.

We lay in the sand, almost stunned from the shock of the fall, me flat on my back with Jean on top of me. He stood above us in the lighted door and laughed.

"Be with you in a minute," he said. "Then we'll get this show on the road." He disappeared back into the shack.

I could feel her struggling against the ropes. Her warm breath was in my face.

"Listen, Jean, there's not much time. Maybe we can make some kind of break, I don't know, but maybe not too, and I want you to know. Ever since I knew I loved you I didn't want to kill him, I only kept on because I thought you did, because I thought you needed me."

I felt her stop moving and then her voice whispered softly. "Was it our wedding night, Harry? That was when it started for me."

"Yes," I said. "But I thought you were just stringing me along. I didn't dream you loved me too."

"I tried not to. I kept thinking about Lucy, and about what we were going to do. But you were so hurt ... so lonely ... I couldn't help it."

"If we had only known ... if we had only told each other ..."

"I know. But I thought you had to kill him to get Lucy and all that out of your mind, to get over what he'd done to you. To be a man again."

"And you were going to help me do that. Make me go through with it."

"Yes. And you were going to help me."

"And neither of us wanted to do it at all."

"No. Not since that night."

"My God," I said. "How can two people get so fouled up?"

We lay there, still and quiet, and even with the sounds of him moving inside, even with the ropes cutting into our flesh, I think we were more at peace than we had ever been. I think we both thought that this was better, to die together and unashamed rather than to kill together and live in fear and shame and regret.

Then something blocked out the light and his shadow fell over us again. He came cautiously down the steps and moved to one side of us. I rolled to the side where I could watch him.

"That sand in the suitcases," he said. "Pretty cute. So I'd think you really were leaving. But I fixed it up in there, all right. It looks like maybe the two of you just stepped out for a walk, the way I fixed it."

He stood there grinning at us and Jean turned her head.

"What are you going to do to us?" she said.

"I'm going to take you for a swim, a nice long swim."

Agonizingly, like lightning in the night, I realized what he was going to do. I had not been the only one to think that Rutherford Millpond would be a good place for murder. I had even thought how easy it would be to hide a body there. That was what he had meant, when he had said he didn't think anybody would ever find us.

And he's probably right, I thought. I doubt if anybody ever will.

"I don't get it," Jean said.

"You will, baby. You will."

He pulled a flashlight from his hip pocket and checked the knot at her back, then snapped it off. He patted her hip and chuckled.

"All right," he said. "On your feet, now. I haven't got all night."

It took us several minutes to make it, but finally we did. He stood there grinning at us all the time. The gun was in his hand again.

"My car's over there in the woods," he said. "Let's go."

That was the hardest journey I ever made, the slow, inching side steps over the deep, clinging sand. I don't know how many times we fell down, but I began to feel bruised all over, the ropes cutting hard into my flesh now, and my arm aching as the circulation went out of it. Worse still was knowing how it must be on her soft arms and body. But she never whimpered.

And always, he was just behind us, grinning, laughing out loud whenever we fell, making filthy remarks if I landed on top. If I get out of this, I thought, just for a minute, just for one minute, I'll stuff that grin down your throat.

Finally we were there and we leaned against the car. He reached through the front window and got a bottle from the seat. He took a long pull at it and wiped his mouth.

"I was pretty smart, eh?" he said. "You thought I'd come driving right up and hand myself over to you." He chuckled. "What a couple of suckers you two turned out to be!"

If you only knew, I thought, what suckers we really are. And you're the biggest of all. Because you could go on and let us go and never hear another word from us the rest of your stinking life. But you're going to kill us and it's going to be for you the way it would have been for us. You're the biggest sucker of all.

He opened the rear door of the car and herded us in. We sprawled all over the back seat, Jean on her side, half on the seat, and I on the floor, my legs twisted up to allow the door to close. Out of the corner of my eye I saw him run his hand along her leg and I kicked savagely at him. He laughed and slammed the door.

He got in and started the engine and drove out into the open and turned the car around. We began to move back along the little road.

Little darts of fear began to shoot through me. This may be all, I thought, this may be the end of everything for us. But it can't! We've got to get out of it, there's a way to get out of it if I could only think of it.

I felt the car sway as we turned onto the bigger road.

"Are you scared?" I whispered.

"Yes. I've never been really scared before. But I am now."

"I am too. He's drinking and he's got a crazy look to him. I never figured him for this. I never thought he had the guts."

She didn't say anything for a long time. We bumped roughly along the road. I figured he must be making about fifty. I could twist my head and see the tops of the tall trees flash by outside.

"I'm sorry," I heard her whisper, almost inaudibly over the sound of the engine. "I'm sorry it's all ending this way."

"Maybe we're not done yet."

"Where is he taking us? What's he going to do with us?"

"The millpond. Where we were going to take him. Only he's going to throw us in, after he shoots us."

She didn't answer for a long time. Then:

"Maybe it's like you said. Maybe it's what we deserve for even thinking about killing him."

"The way you kept egging me on. I thought you only wanted to kill him. I thought ..."

"I know. I wanted you to think so. I thought you'd back out if I didn't keep pushing you. And I thought you had to kill him to be all right again."

"And Lucy. You didn't want to get even for her?"

"Only at first. Then I did. But after that night— I only wanted you and to have you strong again and not going crazy over what she'd done to you."

"It's no good talking about it now," I said. "It's too late now."

"I know. But there's one other thing. What you said about me hating men. That was true too, until that night. But … it was different that time. It hadn't been that way before. Not ever. That night I wanted you to have me."

"I know now. I remember."

We had been jolting along on the big road, toward the millpond, for some time now. I judged we were halfway there.

"Listen," I heard her whisper. "Do you remember about Achilles?"

"This is no time for myths or whatever he was. This is for keeps."

"I know. But remember? Achilles had one weakness. His heel."

"Yes, but I can't …"

"Like Stewart. He has one weakness too."

Then I knew what she meant, what she had in mind. There was no sound from the front seat and we were moving steadily along the bumpy road.

"No," I said. "You don't have to do that."

"I'd do anything, if we could only live, Harry! If we could only be together always."

"So would I. But there must be some other way besides that."

She didn't answer. This is what it's all boiled down to, I thought, two people, two humans, tied together like bundles of old clothes, tossing and bumping and hurting, waiting to die, to feel life go out of them, and thinking, thinking, thinking, aching from the thinking, just trying to find a way to stay alive, to keep on breathing.

And we can't even say it's not our own fault. We can't even say we didn't get ourselves into it. And, God help me, I can't even tell the girl I love, more than I have ever loved anything except maybe life, that I don't want her to use her body on him so we can stay alive. I can't even tell her that.

Because maybe it is the only way. And I want to live. I never wanted to live so much. And I want her to live.

The smooth power of the engine mocked us and we moved on through the blackness. We didn't say anything else. There wasn't anything else to say. But I knew she was lying there against me, aching too from the thinking and the fear and the wanting to live.

I wrenched my body furiously against the ropes that bound us and I heard her gasp in pain.

"I'm sorry," I whispered.

"That's all right. It didn't hurt much."

"Can you move your arms at all?"

"No. Just my legs."

"The bastard. He's fixed us good, all right."

And then I felt the car slow, sliding a little on the dirt, and we turned and slowed even more. Branches slapped against the car and the darkness was closer to us. We've turned off, I thought, we're almost to the pond.

I twisted my head to look out the window. The trees leered at me. Then they were gone and I could see the same old stars and the vast sky and I knew we were on the shore of the pond.

The car braked to a sudden halt, jerking us hard, so that I rolled a little and her weight crushed down harder on me. I heard an oath from the front seat, startled and frightened. The door on the driver's side slammed, and the silence settled down again.

"Where are we?"

"The pond," I whispered. "He must have seen your car."

It seemed a long time that we lay there unmoving, waiting. Then I heard his slow steps crunching over the sand toward us. Here it comes, I thought, it's coming now. I heard her whisper:

"Whatever happens, remember I love you."

The door at my head opened suddenly. The beam of the flash swept into my upturned eyes and I blinked.

"It's a small world," he said. The flash had me blinded but I could almost feel that evil grin across his dark, flushed face. "Imagine finding your car out here. Imagine that."

The flash clicked out. Rough hands went under my shoulders and he began to drag us both from the car. He was breathing hard, he really had to struggle to get the two of us out of there. But he did it. There was another rough, aching jolt against the earth and we lay in the sand at his feet.

"Now the fun begins," he said. "Right where you had it figured to kill me. Yessir. It sure is a small world."

This time he laughed out loud and the echoing lake multiplied it into a hundred voices, mocking and sneering and triumphant.

Chapter Twenty-one

The circulation was almost gone from my arm now and I ached all over from the rough handling and the ropes and the bumpy ride on the hard floor. I could hear her short, quick breathing and I knew it was bad for her too.

He knelt by us and checked the knot at her back again. Quickly he stood away from us and I caught the gleam of starlight on the barrel of the gun.

"Get up," he said. "On your feet."

Again the struggle, the fight to get four feet under us at one time and to push two bodies erect as one. We fell back three times before we made it. I felt the pull of her against me as she swayed on her feet and I quickly leaned against the car, so we would not fall again. We were pulled together like Siamese twins, our backs rigid and our heads forced back.

He went to the door of the car again and got the bottle. Beyond us I could see the bulk of the Chevrolet, where I had parked it that afternoon. And I had thought I hadn't forgotten anything then. A million years ago.

To my right, the pond lay waiting in the starlight. She'll go down in there and never come up, I thought. She will go down under the malignant waters and the weeds will cling to her body and the fish will pass over her in incurious motion and there will never be again the joy of her for anyone. And especially not for me, because I will be with her.

The water was very still, the stumps blacker than ever in the night and the sound of it spilling over the dam clear and unbroken. There's not much time, I thought, there's not much time left.

He backed away from us, about ten feet, and calmly sat down on the sand. He lifted the bottle and took another drink. Let him keep on, I thought. Let him get stone blind and see if I care.

"Now let's talk," he said, his voice a little excited, a little keyed up, but the gun still rocklike in his hand. "Let's talk about you two."

The whisky. It's making his tongue loose. He wants to brag a little, hold it over us a little. And I'm glad. Because that gives us another minute or two to live.

I could feel her body hard against me and I looked down at her and her eyes were already on my face and I was very proud of her. She didn't show the fear that must have been in her and I remembered again the night I had torn her clothes from her and she had disdained to run, but had fought back.

This is a woman, I thought, this is all a woman can be.

His voice sneered at us again:

"That car you brought out here—I could drive it away. But it would be found and that would get them to wondering what had happened to you two."

"Damn right," I said. "You'll never get away with it."

"Maybe not. But I think so. Even if I did it like that, just drove it away, I don't think they could hang it on me. But I have a better idea now. The car being out here gave it to me."

"Look," I said, "for the last time. Just let us go and you'll never have to worry about us again. You don't have to do this."

"Shut up. I'm not going to worry over this thing any more. One hour in bed with a woman isn't worth it. That's all I got—less than that—and it's been keeping me awake nights for two years, worrying about you. I'm through with all that. Especially now I know you were planning to kill me."

"All right. Be a fool, then."

He chuckled.

"Suppose," he said, "I just let them find the car right there where it is now. But they don't find hide or hair of you two. What are they going to think?"

"You tell me. You're doing the talking."

"They'll think you went swimming out here. They'll think maybe this way: Here the two of 'em are, having a swim, only the girl hits her head on something and sinks. Harry dives in to get her out. He gets tangled in the weeds. And they both drown. It's happened before."

I said nothing. I could feel cold fingers around my heart. I heard Jean's breath catch.

"That's better," he said. "Much better than what I had in mind. No gunshots. And then, if they ever do find your bodies, no trying to find out who did it. They'll figure it was an accident."

I still didn't say anything. The cold horror of it was beginning to be almost a tangible thing in me, a hard lump in my belly.

"But I'll need a little co-operation. From both of you."

"I'll be damned if you'll get it. If you think—"

"Shut up," he said. "I can still do it the other way, just shoot you and toss you in with a couple of rocks tied on your feet and drive the car off and ditch it. They won't connect me with it."

"Then do it that way."

"All right. The girl gets it first. In the belly. I'll let you watch her for a little while after I do that, and then maybe I'll work on her face a little bit. With this."

There was a sharp click and the smooth gleam of a switch-blade knife appeared in his hand.

I was sweating freely now. His last words had almost made me sick. I looked at Jean again. She still showed no fear, but even in the night her face was pasty white.

He's crazy, I thought, he's gone right off his rocker. He'd do it. He'd do what he said with that knife.

We had pushed him too far.

"All right," I said. "What do you want us to do?"

He laughed.

"Now that's better. Now you're using your head." He took another pull at the bottle.

"First I'll get her to tie you up, good and tight."

Then he'll have to untie us first, I thought. Maybe we'll have a chance to …

"Then I'll hit her over the head. That'll get her out of the way while I hold your head underwater until you drown. Then I hold her head under too and toss you both in."

"My God!" I said. "You're crazy, man!"

He came to his feet in one smooth, even motion and I saw his lips pull back in a snarl.

"Just be quiet," he said. "Just keep your goddamn mouth shut or you'll get it right now, right where you said you'd give it to me that time."

I knew he meant it, and I remembered he was going to untie us if he went through with the drowning scheme, and I shut up. I didn't even move until I saw him begin to relax.

"All right," he said. "It's either that way or a slug in her belly. Which way?"

"Anything you say. You hold all the cards."

"Damn right. Once I sink the two of you in that lake I won't have anything else to worry about."

"How about the weeds? You'll have to take us down there"—I shuddered—"and tangle us up, so we'll stay. Maybe they'll get you too."

"Not with this." Again the swift gleam of the knife. "Not me. I can't lose tonight."

You lost a long time ago, I thought. And so did I. And so did she. We all lost. None of us ever had a chance after the night you went to Lucy.

"All right," he said. "I'm going to untie you. But remember. I've got the gun and I won't mind shooting it. Not a bit."

"We'll remember."

He came up behind her and I saw the gleam of the knife and felt the rope give as he cut it. In a minute, we were out of it. She slumped wearily away from me, and I let my shoulders relax and stood there flexing my fingers, trying to get the circulation back into them. Needles of fire flared up my arm.

"Now," he said. "I'm sorry I can't furnish bathing suits. I guess you'll have to take your clothes off to make it look right. Both of you."

We looked at each other dumbly.

"Don't worry," he sneered. "You got a lot more to worry about than your modesty."

No, I thought, modesty doesn't mean anything now. Nothing does, but staying alive, even just for one minute.

I started taking my clothes off. He stood over ten feet away, the gun steady, the knife in his other hand, sneering a little. His eyes kept flicking greedily toward Jean.

It's funny, I thought, I ought to hate him. I used to hate him. But it's different now. I have known what it is to feel that you have to kill, that there isn't anything else to do. I have known that and I cannot hate even him for feeling the same way. Not even him.

But I kept watching him for the slip, for the moment of hesitation, for the time when the gun would drop, when he would take his eyes off me long enough.

I was undressed now, standing there stark naked, and I turned my head and so was she. The starlight spilled over her slim, pale body, and the moon, peeping now over the trees on the far side of the lake, cast a golden glow over the high, small breasts and the fine, slender legs and the rounded hips.

I looked back at Stewart. He was licking his lips and I saw that his eyes were not on me at all now, but were gorging themselves on her.

I took a slow step to the left, away from her. Instantly the gun swiveled at me and the flushed face swung toward me, anger lighting it all over.

"Look at me, Dick. Look at me."

Her voice was husky and low and I felt a chill go down my spine. He didn't look away from my face. But I turned my head and looked at her.

She was holding her arms out to him, swaying a little, moving her hips ever so slightly. Her voice beckoned him again:

"Look at all of me," she said.

His gun was still very steady on me, but his eyes now switched back and forth quickly between us.

She took a step forward.

"You stand still," he said.

She stopped. He licked his lips again and shook his head. She ran her hands sensuously over her breasts and down her flanks. The hips moved again.

It almost made me sick to watch, to see her having to do this to herself in front of him. But I loved her for it, because I knew it was for me. For us.

I took another step to the side. The gun did not fol low me.

"You could have me," she said. "You don't have to kill me."

"You stop that. Don't you come any closer."

She took another step forward. His eyes were all for her now, but I was still too far away to rush him. I moved a little more, angling for his side, away from her. Just keep your eyes on her, I thought, just don't notice me moving at all. Just forget I'm here and keep looking at her.

"Kill him," she said. "I'll help you. I'll help you hold his head under. But don't kill me."

"You bitch," he almost whispered. The gun pointed between us now, at nothing. I saw it tremble slightly and his eyes were glued to her body. I moved a little more. One more step was all I needed, and she was buying it.

A breeze was moving across the dark water and I felt it chill my bare skin where sweat had bathed it.

She had swayed very close to him now, still moving her hands over her breasts and stomach and hips.

"Look at me. You can have all of me … all of me…."

And then I had taken that last step I needed. The gun still aimed at space and his face, oblivious now of all but her pale, gleaming body, swaying slowly before him, offered up to him, was avid with desire and lust.

"Yeah," he said. "Yeah, I could have you…."

I dug my toes into the sand and leaped at his legs and felt myself driven through space, propelled, it seemed, for an eternity of waiting, of listening for the roar, of almost feeling the bullet smack into me, the hard smash of it, and then there was the good, clean shock of my shoulder driving into his thigh, of the giving of it, the collapse of it, and the sand gritting against my face, and the shape of him under me, and the strength coming up out of my belly to fight.

I grabbed blindly for his arm and felt my fingers close down on his wrist. Whisky breath fumed in my face. His body convulsed violently and he twisted from under me.

I was on my side, holding desperately to the arm that held the gun and trying to get my knee between his legs. He got a leg under him and half rose and I saw the long blade of the knife sweeping at me.

I rolled into him, hard, and felt something sear across the top of my left shoulder. For a moment we were almost face to face, and I saw the other arm go back again, the switch blade shining in his hand, and I thought, Here it comes now, here comes the end of it.

And then he grunted sharply in my ear, and I felt his weight jerked back from me, and I turned my head and saw her standing there, her legs wide and braced, both hands clutched around his wrist.

I was holding his left arm to the ground, pinned with my arm and body, and she was pulling now on his right, ripping it back from the socket, her whole face clenched in the strain of it, the knife poised in his fingers, and then he screamed once from the pain of it and his hand opened and the knife fell from it.

She let go his arm and her hand went swiftly to the ground and I saw her straighten and step away, holding the knife in her hand. His whole weight came on top of me again, stale breath sighing out of him, and I felt his now free fist punch sharply at my kidneys.

If I only had two arms, I thought, if I could only hold on to this wrist and still have an arm left to fight with instead of a goddamned useless stump hanging off a useless shoulder …

I rolled again, gouging my head and shoulder and stump into his chest, and came up on top of him, still holding down the hand that held the gun. He's strong, I thought. I've got to get my arm free. He was exerting all his strength there now, trying to force the gun back up toward me, warding off my knee with his own, squeezing at my throat with his other hand.

Suddenly I let my arm go limp and the fierce strength of his own arm, the one holding the gun, snapped our locked wrists up into mid-air.

Then, with all the force I could gather, I shot my arm straight ahead, still gripping his wrist.

I could almost feel the bones grind in his shoulder socket, and he groaned hoarsely and I snapped the arm against the earth and twisted his wrist steadily to the inside.

He opened his mouth to scream, his body writhing under me, and I rammed my shoulder into his face and ground it against his nose.

"Drop it," I said. "Drop the gun or I'll tear your arm right off your shoulder!"

I felt the strength of him gather under me for a last effort, I felt all of him bunch into a hard knot, coiled, ready to unwind in one jolting, twisting smash. I hung on and then it came from under me, the animal thrash and fury of it, and I took it, grunting hard from the shock, and still hung on.

Then he was spent, and I knew it and twisted harder on his wrist until, finally, with a despairing anguished shriek like that of a wounded beast, his fingers relaxed and the gun fell from them.

Now, I thought. Now. It's just him and me. No guns, no nothing. Just his muscles and mine and nothing else, the way it should have been all the time.

I let go of his arm and grabbed the gun. I felt my feet under me and sprang away from him.

Chapter Twenty-two

She was beside me quickly and we stood there looking down at him, snarling and defiant on the earth, his hair wild and tangled, the eyes blazing and the lips pulled back, his shirt half torn from him, the calm water shining unruffled behind him.

I remembered that Jean and I were naked. I turned my head slightly toward her. She stood quietly, her breasts heaving a little, her legs slightly bent, pale beauty standing unafraid beside me.

"Put some clothes on," I said.

She looked at me and her eyes went to my shoulder. I remembered the fiery sweep of the knife against it.

"You're hurt. You're bleeding."

"Not much. He just scratched me with the knife. Put something on, baby."

She moved toward the car, where our clothes lay. I looked steadily at Stewart, holding the gun on him. He lay there and you could see the tension crouching, coiled in him. Neither of us moved.

Then she was beside me again and I saw from the corner of my eye that she was buttoning my shirt around her. It reached almost to her knees.

"I ought to bandage that shoulder."

"Later. It's all right."

His voice flung up at us from the ground, high-pitched now, more evil than ever.

"What are you going to do?"

"In a little while," I said, "we're going to call the Sheriff. We're going to tell him the whole story."

He laughed, the sound moist in his throat.

"Even what you were going to do to me?"

"Even that."

"And how are you going to prove anything on me?"

"Easy," I said. "Because I'll do the calling, not you. Because this is your gun, not mine. That's

your knife, not mine. And there aren't any rope
burns on you. Like on Jean and me, where you tied
our arms."

His malevolent eyes narrowed at each word.

"They'll find out all about the other time," he
said. "About Lucy."

"That's right," I said.

"You haven't got the guts!"

"Guts are funny," I said. "It's easy to have guts
when you hold the whip hand. Jean, hand me that
knife."

I heard her breath catch, then felt the knife
pressed into my hand. She took the gun and held it
steadily on Stewart. I flicked the long blade open. I
held it carelessly and his eyes shifted quickly
toward it.

"What happened that night?" I said. "What
really happened?"

His laugh was a little uneasy, but still ugly.

"I want to know, Stewart. And I want to know
quick. You gave me some ideas about this knife."

He eyed me narrowly and said nothing.

Quickly I dropped to one knee beside him and
the point of the knife touched his throat.

"What happened that night?" I said.

His eyes flicked from side to side and his tongue
darted at his dry lips. I pushed the knife a little
harder at his throat.

"There was a letter," he burst out, the words
high and weak, hurrying out of his throat. "The
envelope had a return address for some adoption
outfit up north. When it came through the post
office I saw it ... and opened it. It told about how
her baby had been adopted."

"And you blackmailed her. Threatened to tell
me."

"Well, I ..."

"And all you wanted was just to go to bed with
her?"

"Listen, Harry, don't ..."

"And you knew she'd do it, didn't you? To keep me from finding out."

"I—Yes. But you got to ..."

I stood up and backed away.

"I'm going to beat the living hell out of you," I said.

I heard Jean gasp. His eyes narrowed and I saw his muscles gathering. I handed the knife to Jean.

"Get up," I said. "It's just you and me now."

The coiled tension in him jerked him to his feet in one explosive motion.

"Harry," Jean said, "you can't—"

"I've got to."

And then he laughed.

"Come on," he said. "Come on and finish it."

And I remembered my arm again, suddenly, blindingly, and cursed myself for male vanity and conceit in thinking I could do it, in thinking I could stand there and slug it out with him, with both of his strong arms, and win. I cursed myself and knew that I had to do it anyway.

I stepped quickly forward and telegraphed a wild, swinging right toward his chin and saw him begin to duck and swung my right leg up, as if I were drop-kicking a football.

My foot caught him in the chest and he straightened up, grunting, off balance, surprise all over his face. I clubbed him with the right. He went down in a heap on the ground.

This is no time for fair fighting, I thought. The hell with the rules. I swung my foot hard into his ribs.

He rolled with it and I felt his hands go around my leg and yank. I hopped a step or two forward and he pulled again and I went down, sprawling at full length, my head not a yard from the edge of the dam.

He sprang at me from the earth and I felt his full weight come down on my back, his hands go under my chin, and my head snap back.

I felt bones rub together in my neck and shoulders.

"I'll break your sonafabitching neck," I heard him mutter in my ear. I thrashed behind me with my one arm, but I couldn't reach him.

"You'll never tell, London! Never. I'll kill you—just like I killed Lucy."

Something exploded in me.

I humped my back sharply and sprang forward to my knees like a bucking horse. He flung over my shoulders in front of me and I ground my feet into the earth and drove into him again, furious now, forgetting all but the hatefulness of him, all but what he had said, and suddenly felt space open up beneath us, and remembered, with sharp revolting fear, and felt the shock of the water, the cold awakening surprise of it, the evil blackness of it, closing around us.

The water quieted us both and for a moment we sank easily and swiftly, my arm still around his waist, the force of our fall driving us deep below the surface.

And then his body, slippery now in the murky water, moved violently against me and I felt him slip out of my grasp, his legs churning heavily in the water, smashing into my stomach as he began to rise toward the surface.

I began to kick too, a deep fear of being alone down there shooting through me, a fear of the silence and the blackness and the evil under the surface of the calm lake, my lungs beginning to burn now and my eyes stinging from the one time I had opened them under the water.

My head broke above the surface and I drew in great gulps of air. I heard her scream. His arms closed around my neck from behind, hard.

The sweet breath choked out of me. Before I could resist we were underwater again, sinking slowly now, my empty lungs giving me no buoyancy, my heart pounding heavily, and his arms like two boa constrictors around my throat.

I felt my whole head popping and I tugged at the arms around my throat. They were of steel. Down we sank, farther into the blackness, the pressure heavy on us now, little bubbles tickling about us, and the water silent, unmoving, imprisoning us both.

I thrashed hard at him, but now his legs squeezed tightly around my waist and his grip seemed to grow stronger. Got me now, I thought, got me good unless I can hold my breath longer. Got to hold my breath....

Then I felt the first tentative licking of the long waving weeds reaching out for me, reaching for him too. Pure terror filled all of me, terror for something unhuman that waited for us there, yearned for us, would never let us go.

I jerked frantically, my whole chest bursting now for the want of oxygen, my head feeling a yard wide, my nostrils burning, my feet frozen up under me, as far as possible from the hungry, terrible tentacles reaching for them.

I felt his grip relax.

I twisted my body madly. I felt his legs slip away from my waist. My fingers clawed at his arm.

I did it. I outlasted him.

My feet kicked once, twice. I dug at the water with my arm, straining every muscle in me, and felt my body rising in the water, rising, rising, still bursting for air, but rising now, rising forever, and then there was the blessed, the unbearable sweetness of the air on my skin and the deep fire of it entering my parched lungs in great gulps and the fuzzy tiredness inside my head and the popping in my eyes and ears.

"Harry!"

I felt a hand grasp my hair and pull me toward the dam and I twisted up my head and her face was right over mine, her eyes wide and her mouth strained in the effort, as she lay flat on her stomach, holding me up by my hair.

"You can reach the bank! Put out your hand, Harry!"

I put out my hand, obedient as a child, too tired to think for myself, and felt the rough stone of the dam under me. My weight rode easily in the water then, and I felt her hand let go of my hair, and I clung there, spent.

I felt her hand on my cheek.

"You were down there so long, Harry. I thought you'd never come up. It was so black...."

Thought began to come back into my head, to move cautiously around in my brain like a cat nosing at food, and I nodded wearily.

"Stewart. Where is he?"

"He hasn't come up."

I shook my head. A great weight seemed to be on my shoulders. He hasn't come up, I thought. That means he's still down there. Now, isn't that silly? If he hasn't come up, of course he's ...

... still down there!

"The weeds," I said. "The weeds got him."

I hadn't outlasted him after all. Only the weeds had defeated him.

"But you came up, Harry. You came up!"

"Give me the knife."

"The knife?"

"Got to get him up. Can't let him die now. Give it here."

"No, Harry, you might—"

"No time to talk. Give it to me. Got to get him up."

I felt the haft of the knife slip under my fingers, still clinging to the stone dam. Then her hand was on mine for a moment, soft and strong and smooth.

"Harry, come back to me."

I let go of the dam and put a foot against it and pushed myself away from it. The third time, I thought; they say you don't come up after the third time you go down.

I took several long breaths and then a final one and closed my eyes. I went under in a surface dive, my one arm, its hand holding the knife, pulling me down, the cool, dark waters slipping over me with oily ease.

I opened my eyes.

It's dark down here.

It's dark and I am afraid.

But I will not let another man die down here, no matter who he is, no matter how afraid I am, if I can get him out. Because he must want to live too, and I know what it is to want to live. Wanting to kill is nothing beside wanting to live.

The water is heavy. The water is crushing me.

And I can't see. I open my eyes and it is as if I had no eyes, only the stinging tells me they are there. If I could only see.

Down, down, down. Dark. Cold now.

I feel it. I feel the first touch of it, undulant against me, and then another, and now I am into them, they are all about me, their touch slides over me, and I am swimming into them. Their long, slimy fingers are caressing me, loving me, closing over me.

My chest burns. My lungs are on fire.

Something cold. Slick. I can't see but I feel it.

An arm. I slide my fingers along it and there is a shoulder, the arm straight out from it.

I am trying to forget the soft waving things, coming at me out of the dark, the deep. I am trying to forget them.

I can't forget them.

Now I touch his body and it is free, it is parallel and still in the water, it must be his other arm they have caught. My hand is on it now, sliding down it and ... yes. Yes.

Around his wrist. Wound and enmeshed and bound. The knife.

Slash. Slash.

If I could only see, if only my lungs were not bursting in me, my chest on fire, all of me swelling and ballooning and screaming for oxygen.

Slash. And then upward.

She got us both out.

On the soft, crunching sand, crouched there clad only in my shirt, desperate, fear-stricken, she got us out.

She hauled him first, then me, up on the sand. I could hear her doing it, see her finally, but there were no muscles in me to help.

But she did it. Somehow.

I lay there, my legs still in the water, my body jackknifed over the edge of the dam, and felt her hands, anxious on my body.

"No. I'm all right. Him. Pump him."

"Harry ..."

Then for a long time nothing but the lying there, still and peaceful, not having to move, only having to breathe, only having to worship breath. Not even having to think.

But slowly it all came back.

I lifted my head. A few feet away, she knelt over him. He was sprawled on the sand, very limp and still. Her body, my shirt clinging wetly to it, straddling him, bent rhythmically down and back, her arms extended to his waist. Her breath went out of her in a little grunt with each pressure stroke, but there were no breaks in her movements.

I heaved myself farther up on the bank. The wet sand clung like a mat to my naked chest. Her head turned toward me, but the pumping went on.

I walked over to the car and put on my clothes, the sand gritty inside of them, and went back to her side and sat down.

"Is he alive?"

"I don't know. He hasn't moved."

"He's got to live."

"Yes."

"Keep pumping him. Maybe I can help in a little while."

His head was turned sideways on one flaccid arm, his mouth open, water drooling from it to the sand. She leaned forward on him again and his body gave with her pressure.

He's got to live, I thought.

"Did you hear him, Jean? He said he killed Lucy. And I thought I had done it ... all this time. Did you hear him?"

"I heard him. He almost killed you too."

Her eyes were naked in relief and slowly passing fear and I reached out and touched her shoulder, leaving my hand there as her body bent to the pumping.

"He tried to frame it on me. He killed her and he put the gun in my hand and left me there like that."

"Why, Harry? Why did he kill her?"

"So he'd be safe. So I couldn't prove he'd been there and so I would go to the chair and wouldn't be able to kill him. So he could hang on to that wife and that store and all that money."

"And when you fooled them with the suicide note and shooting yourself, he must have known that someday he'd have to kill you, to keep it from ever being found out."

"Yes. He must have been thinking that all the time. Just like I was. Maybe he even thought I knew he had killed her. Only I went off the track and for a while he thought he wouldn't have to. Then you came along and we forced the whole thing to a head."

"So all that time he was planning to kill you too."

"Yes."

So he is no worse than I am. Or than I was. Because I was lucky. I found out in time. I found out you have to live with yourself too. And I guess he never did.

I could see she was tiring now. I longed to put my arm around her and hold her, hold her forever.

"I'll try it a while," I said.

"It wouldn't work. You need both hands."

"I hate to see you wear yourself out."

"It's worth it. Like you said, he's got to live."

"Yes. So we can turn Brax Jordan loose on him and get him to tell how Lucy died. So the law can make him pay for it. I think he'll talk. After tonight, I think he will."

She sighed at me again, still bending steadily to the pumping.

"That wasn't why you pulled him out of there, Harry. It's important, but that wasn't why you went down in that water to get him."

"Maybe not. I don't know."

"It was because now you don't want anyone to die."

I didn't say anything.

"Well, I don't either. That's why I don't mind doing this."

I reached for his wrist and tried to find a pulse.

"I don't know. I don't feel anything."

"He'll live," she said. "I'll make him."

And again I knew how implacable she could be, how she could will herself to do anything, anything.

"What about us?" she said.

"You haven't done anything. When he hears about tonight, Walt—the Sheriff—will forget what we planned to do. And all they can get me for on the other thing is covering it up, making it look like suicide. I don't think he'll care too much about that, either. Not if he gets the real murderer."

She looked at the stump of my arm.

"You've already paid for that, anyway," she said.

I don't know how long we remained there like that. I don't know how long it was that her small, unrelenting body bent ceaselessly to his, willing life back to him, forcing him to live again, forcing him to return from death to life.

I don't know how tired she must have been, her arms numb and aching, her back screaming in despair, the muscles of her smooth and tender flesh drawn into open sores of fatigue, and her mind and her proud, undefeatable heart forbidding her to quit.

I only know that it was a long time, that the moon moved high, that the stars winked on, and that I had all the time in the world to think, to dream, to know inside of me what lay ahead for us forever.

And then I heard him cough.

Without speaking, I stood up. She had not by one movement broken her rhythm. I thought how it was almost like birth, how that too gave life in straining muscles and grinding fatigue and agonizing rhythm. God did not give life lightly. Somebody had to suffer for it.

Maybe that's one reason why it's so precious.

"He's alive," I said.

"Yes. You'd better go call the Sheriff now. I'll be all right. He's weak as a fish, and besides, I've got the gun."

I bent and kissed the back of her neck.

"And then I'll come back," I said. "And we'll be together always."

The moon shone no more brightly than her eyes.

I walked over to her car and got in and drove into the narrow little road and onto the bigger one and pretty soon I saw the lights of the little filling station from which I would call the Sheriff.

All of a sudden, I thought about Lucy. If there were any such thing as revenge, she had it now. But that didn't matter, never had mattered. What was important was that she had not betrayed me, had not betrayed anybody, and that now she could rest peacefully, knowing that I knew she had died to save me from hurt and shame and my own violence.

Lucy, I thought, I'm sorry. That was the only time I ever doubted you. And I'm sorry.

And somehow I knew too that she would be glad Jean was with me now, and would be with me forever. I believe that's the way she would have wanted it, I thought. I believe she would have wanted Jean to have all that was taken from her.

And only then I remembered that I had not yet told Jean about the money Brax Jordan held for me.

I chuckled.

It will make a nice down payment on a farm, I thought. One like she's always wanted.

THE END

Paul Connolly/Tom Wicker Bibliography
(1926-2011)

NOVELS as Paul Connolly

Get out of Town (Gold Medal, 1951)
Tears Are for Angels (Gold Medal, 1952)
So Fair, So Evil (Gold Medal, 1955)

NOVELS as Tom Wicker

The Kingpin (Sloane, 1953)
The Devil Must (Harper, 1957)
The Judgment (Morrow, 1961)
Facing the Lions (Viking, 1973)
Unto This Hour (Viking, 1984)
Donovan's Wife (Morrow, 1992)
Easter Lilly: A Novel of the South Today (Morrow, 1998)

NONFICTION

Kennedy Without Tears, the Man Beneath the Myth (Morrow, 1964)
JFK and LBJ: The Influence of Personality Upon Politics (Morrow, 1968)
A Time to Die (Quadrangle, 1975; reprinted as A Time to Die: The Attica Prison Revolt, University of Nebraska Press, 1994)
On Press (Viking, 1978)
One of Us: Richard Nixon and the American Dream (Random House, 1991)
Tragic Failure: Racial Integration in America (Morrow, 1996)

Indictment: The News Media and the Criminal
    Justice System (With Wallace Westfeldt; First
    Amendment Center, 1998)

The Nixon Years, 1969-1974: White House to
    Watergate (Abbeville Press, 1999)

Dwight D. Eisenhower (Times Books, 2002)

On the Record: An Insider's Guide to Journalism
    (Bedford/St. Martin's, 2002)

George Herbert Walker Bush (Lipper/Viking,
    2004)

Shooting Star: The Brief Arc of Joe McCarthy
    (Harcourt, 2006)

Paul Connolly is the pseudonym of American journalist Thomas Grey "Tom" Wicker. Born in Hamlet, North Carolina on June  18, 1926, he graduated from the University of North Carolina and won a Neiman Fellowship at Harvard University in 1957. Wicker is best known as a political reporter and columnist for *The New York Times*, which he joined in the early 1950s, but at the same time he wrote three pulp novels for Gold Medal Books as Paul Connolly. After that, he wrote another seven novels as Tom Wicker as well as a series of political histories about U.S. presidents. In 1975, he won an Edgar Award for Best Fact Crime Book for *A Time to Die: The Attica Prison Revolt*. Wicker also wrote the *Times* lead story about the assassination of President Kennedy, having ridden in the Dallas motorcade that accompanied him. He died from an apparent heart attack on November 25, 2011.

Black Gat Books

Black Gat Books is a new line of mass market paperbacks introduced in 2015 by Stark House Press. New titles appear every three months, featuring the best in crime fiction reprints. Each book is size to 4.25" x 7", just like they used to be. Collect them all.

Stark House Press
1315 H Street, Eureka, CA 95501 707-498-3135
griffinskye3@sbcglobal.net   www.starkhousepress.com
Available from your local bookstore or direct from the
publisher.